HIS SECRETARY'S LITTLE SECRET

BY
CATHERINE MANN

MILLS & BOON

First Published in Great Britain 2016
By Mills & Boon, an imprint of HarperCollins*Publishers*
1 London Bridge Street, London, SE1 9GF

© 2016 Catherine Mann

ISBN: 978-0-263-91884-7

51-1116

USA TODAY bestselling and RITA® Award–winning author **Catherine Mann** has penned over fifty novels, released in more than twenty countries. After years as a military spouse moving around the country bringing up four children, Catherine has settled in her home state of South Carolina. The nest didn't stay empty long, though, as Catherine is an active member of the board of directors for the Sunshine State Animal Rescue. For more information, visit www.catherinemann.com.

To my animal rescue pals everywhere—especially Virginia, Sharon and Tiffany. You bring such talent, joy and support to this emotional journey!

One

Portia Soto's mama always said doctors didn't grow on trees. That an exotic name couldn't make up for her plain looks. And to count her blessings if she got a proposal from a podiatrist twice her age.

Clearly, Portia's mama hadn't counted on her daughter ever sitting beneath a towering palm watching Dr. Easton Lourdes hang upside down by his knees as he tried to save an ivory-billed woodpecker. An endangered species and thus warranting the wildlife preserve veterinarian's full attention. Which was convenient, since that meant he wouldn't notice he'd totally captured Portia's.

Between the branches of the ancient black mangrove, small stars winked into her vision, the lingering violet of sunset fading into black. The moments just after sunset in the wildlife preserve were Portia's favorite. Night birds trilled overlapping tunes through the dense, steamy woods. Everything seemed somehow prettier, more lush and flamboyant in the absence of sunlight—the preserve transformed into a decadent Eden. At night, the place was a mysterious beauty, far more enticing than Portia had ever considered herself to be.

Except she didn't feel much like herself when she was around Dr. Lourdes.

To be frank, Easton was hot. Really hot. Sexy in a shaggy-haired, unconventional way. An extremely wealthy heir to a family fortune, and a genius veterinarian with a specialty in exotic animals.

He also happened to be the unsuspecting father of Portia's unborn baby, thanks to one impulsive night during a tropical storm nearly two months ago.

In the time that had passed since their unplanned hookup, she'd done her best to put their relationship back on a professional level, to safeguard her hard-won space and independence. A task that had been increasingly difficult to stick to, what with him casting steamy, pensive looks her way when he thought she wasn't aware.

But wow, was she ever aware of him. Always.

So apparently, for Portia, doctors did grow on trees. But that didn't stop the chaos overtaking her life in spite of her best efforts to carefully organize and control her world. She wanted to figure out her plan for the future before she told her onetime lover about their baby. But she was running out of time.

They'd had an impulsive encounter during the stress and fear of being in close quarters during a tropical storm. Such an atypical thing for her to do—have a one-night stand, much less a one-night stand with her boss. She'd always followed the rules, and she'd denied her attraction to Easton until the tension of that tumultuous frightful storm had led her to give in.

She'd enjoyed every moment of that night, but the next morning she'd freaked out. She'd worried about putting her much-needed job and on-site housing in jeopardy—and about how intensely being with Easton had moved her. She didn't have time for messy emotions, much less a relationship. She'd been living day to day, working to keep her head above water financially, especially since her brother had started college four years ago.

Now she had no choice but to think about the future for her child. Her need to establish her independence had to be placed on the fast track for her child's sake. She refused to let her baby have the unsure life she herself had lived through because of her parents' lack of any care or planning for their children's welfare.

The thought of the future nudged Portia into movement. A small movement, of course. It wasn't as if she could just run out of here and leave her boss without the spotlight she was holding. Her hand fell to her still smooth stomach covered by a loose T-shirt layered over trim cargo shorts—her fieldwork basics. Neatly pressed, of course.

A leaf plummeted to the ground with surprising speed. Ten more fell down from the limb above her head, reminding Portia to pay attention to the man above her.

"Can you adjust the spotlight to the left?"

"Sure, how far?"

"To the left."

Ah, nice and vague. Her favorite sort of directions. "Four inches? Twelve inches?"

"Move and I'll tell you when to stop."

"That works—" Portia checked her response. She'd

been second-guessing herself more than ever since that night. Things that hadn't bothered her before now suddenly worried her.

"Stop."

Four inches. She'd moved four flipping inches. How much easier would it have been for him to say that?

She sighed. She was irritable, nauseated and her swollen breasts hurt like crazy. She needed a new bra ASAP. Under cover of the dark, she repositioned one poking end away from her tender flesh. "Can you see now?"

"Almost got it. Just have to stretch farther."

The syllables also stretched, just as she imagined his fingers were doing. Always dramatic. Which was part of his allure...

A cracking sound popped through the night. Portia looked up into the twisted web of branches, her eyes desperately trying to process the image before her. She watched Easton fall out of the black mangrove in what felt like slow motion. He was a silhouetted rush of leaves and flailing limbs, culminating in an echoing thud as he hit the ground. The chorus of nighttime birds stopped as if they too were interested in the doctor's fate.

Panic filled her veins. Her feet and hands grew numb but she pushed them into motion. Fast.

He didn't move, and from her distance, she couldn't see if his chest rose and fell. "Easton!"

His name was a plea and a command to answer all at once. His limbs were splayed out inches from the tree trunk. He'd barely missed landing on the protruding roots. From the muted light, it looked like he had barely avoided impaling himself on a decaying tree limb.

She closed in on him, crouched down to examine him.

Thank the Lord, he was breathing. She felt his pulse. It was strong, but he didn't respond to her touch.

Laying a hand on his shoulder, she gently shook him. Wanting him to be okay. Needing him to be okay. The thought of him hurt sent her mind tumbling into the land of what-if? She'd become adequate at shoving the big what-ifs aside, but with the father of her future child lying unconscious, worst-case scenarios flooded her mind.

What if she didn't get to tell him about the baby? What if he was in a coma? What if…

What if his eyes—sharp blue as lapis lazuli—opened and he continued to look at her like *that*? Her wild thoughts halted as she saw his mischievous gaze trace her outline in the dark.

"I'm alright but don't let that make you move," he muttered, the right corner of his lips pulling up with sexy confidence.

His dark hair curled around his neck—twigs and branches adorning his head like the crown of some mythical forest prince. A sexy prince at that. Her hand lingered on his wrist, making her recall the night they'd spent together. The way he'd held her. She had carefully avoided his touch since they'd woken up to safety and a return to their normal working relationship—since finding out she carried his baby. Everything felt complicated.

She wanted to bolt away. Pushing her back into the neighboring Florida buttonwood tree, she swallowed hard. She didn't know how much longer she could keep her job, living in her cabana on the refuge, and hide the truth. There just wasn't time to save all the money she would need to be independent before the truth became obvious. The panic nearly made her lose her breath, but she pushed it aside as she'd been doing for weeks.

Yes, she would tell him. He deserved to know. But she wanted to get through that initial doctor's appointment first, and each day gave her more time to organize her thoughts into the best way to balance this scary turn her life had taken.

A turn of events made all the more difficult by the way her body remembered too well the explosive passion they'd shared. Even thinking about that night, with the feel and scent of him so close now, turned her inside out with want.

He rested on his back, watching her with those clear blue eyes as he stroked a loose strand of her hair. "Damn, you're a pretty woman."

"Stop. You don't mean it." Why had she said that? It was as good as asking for another compliment and she'd sworn to herself she wouldn't spend her life wrapped up in appearances as her beauty queen mother had.

His gaze held hers and refused to let go. "Don't I?"

"Maybe you do in your own way. But you're a flirt. Get your mind on business. How's the bird?"

Though the movement made him wince, he straightened, sitting up. He had managed to protect the fragile bird during his fall. Easton held it proudly as it nestled into his hand. "Not a mark on him—not from the fall, anyway. We should get back to the clinic and figure out why he's unable to fly."

"I'll drive. Unless you object, but you really shouldn't," she couldn't stop herself from babbling, "since you did just fall from a tree."

He shrugged, rising slowly to his feet. "Of course you can drive. Why would I have a problem with your driving?"

"Most men prefer to drive." Her father always had, declaring her mother too airheaded to be trusted behind the wheel. Scrunching her nose at the memory, Portia stood, dusting off the leaves that clung to her pants.

"I'm not most men. And you're right. I did just fall out of a tree." He shed more small twigs as they made their way to the sanctuary's four-door truck.

"Then it's settled. I'll take the wheel." Driving the massive vehicle would allow her some element of control. And damn, did she need that in spades right now.

"You're a better driver than I am anyway, even when I haven't backflipped down a few limbs to land on my ass."

"Okay, seriously, I can't think of another man on the planet who would admit that." As her head moved, a strand of her normally perfectly pulled-back hair caught on her eyelash. On instinct, her hand flew upward, folding it back into her ponytail. Back to order.

He grinned roguishly. "Then they must not have my confidence."

Her eyebrows lifted. "Or arrogance."

"True." He slid into the passenger side. "You asked for an appointment with me earlier and then the emergency call came in about the ivory-billed woodpecker. We'll have some time to talk on the drive back. What did you wish to speak about?"

Telling him about her pregnancy like this? Not at all what she planned. Not at all what she would do. When she told him, it'd be in a calm setting. One of her choosing. Not in the company of a wild, injured animal. Or a wildly sexy, injured man. "This isn't the time."

"Why not? Is it that serious? If so, speak up now," he said firmly, turning to face her. Those blue eyes demanding something of her.

"Let's take care of business first." Her lips thinned into a line. Pushing him away. Her mother had depended on a man for everything and then had nothing when that man died bankrupt in prison. Portia had vowed she wouldn't let herself commit to anyone until she was certain she could stand on her two feet, debt free and independent. She wouldn't let herself think about how much harder that would be as a single mother.

His eyes narrowed and she could practically see him running through a catalog of possible topics.

"It's personal?" he asked.

"That's not what I said."

"About the night of the tropical storm six weeks ago—" A hungry smile pushed along his mouth.

Damn him for being so intuitive. He had a knack for that. All the more reason for her to be carefully guarded around him.

"Let's not speak about that now."

"You haven't wanted to speak of it since the storm. When are we ever going to talk about it? You're a determined woman, that's for certain."

She knew she couldn't delay the conversation forever, but right now her stomach was still in turmoil over his fall. And she wanted to go to her first doctor's appointment to confirm that the pregnancy was on track before turning her whole world upside down.

And yes, she was trying to think of any reason she could to delay, because once she told Easton about his baby, she would lose control of her life forever.

Dr. Easton Lourdes leaned his seat halfway back, his head still spinning. Partly from the fall, but mostly from the woman beside him and the memory of those moments he'd kept his eyes closed and just absorbed the feel of her against him. Since she'd come to work with him two years ago, he'd suspected there were fires burning behind her uptight demeanor. But hell, he'd had no idea how hot they'd blaze until that one night with her during the storm.

Portia Soto. The most organized secretary on the planet. The woman who—until recently—had kept his eccentric spirit in line. Until their night of passion during a tropical storm showed him just how wild she could be once she let down that tightly upswept hair.

But the next day, she'd gathered her long caramel-brown hair back as fiercely as ever. Tighter even.

He needed his secretary. The Lourdes Family Wildlife Refuge was fast becoming an internationally renowned animal research and rescue center, and he was the man in charge of the science. To make the impact he wanted to make on the world, he *needed* his secretary. But he wanted Portia. And he wasn't sure how to have both.

If only he understood humans as well as he did animals. His childhood spent with rich, globe-trotting parents had exposed him to creatures around the world. He'd paid attention and taken in an understanding of animals' unspoken language. But even though he'd had the best of everything money could buy, he'd lacked much in the way of learning how to make connections with people other than his parents and his older brother. No sooner than he'd make a friend, his family would pack up and jet off to another exotic locale.

Easton cracked his neck, a crescendo of echoing pops responded in his back, the tension finally unwinding. With his neck less contracted, he positioned himself so he could watch her. Portia's gel manicured nails were still quite perfect as she gripped the pickup truck's steering wheel at a "nine and three" position that would make any driver's ed teacher proud. Her doe-brown eyes were focused, attentive to the road.

Intentional. That was how he'd describe Portia. Intentional and proper.

With all her wildness contained.

Despite her manicured look, she fit in well at the wildlife preserve his family owned and funded. Easton brought his world-renowned skills as a veterinarian/scientist specializing in exotic animals. His brother, Xander, ran the family business and fund-raising.

And there sure as hell was a lot of fund-raising and political maneuvering involved in saving animals. P ortia's calm organizational skills were an immeasurable asset on that front too, according to his brother, Xander. Easton only had to show up in a tux every few months and talk about the research he loved.

For the most part, he spent his time handling the hands-on rescue and research efforts, and Portia's efficiency helped him make that happen. He was lucky his family's wealth meant he could leave the fund-raising to his brother and get his hands dirty doing what he enjoyed most.

And he tried his damnedest to entice Portia to play in the dirt with him.

Easton's eyes slid from her face to the soft, yellow lights on the road back to the clinic. The preserve stretched for a few acres on Key Largo, a small island in the archipelago south of Florida. A necessary answer to urbanization and tourist development, Easton believed, as did his new board of directors, apparently.

He was damn lucky. He lived his dream every day. Sure, some people were able to turn passion into a paycheck, but Easton was a veterinarian at his preserve solely for passion. He recognized that he'd been blessed by his family's money. It had enabled him to follow his vocation without worrying about compensation. He didn't advertise his lack of salary because, for Easton, it didn't matter. He felt honored to work for the sole purpose of helping the animals. To do some good in this world. Money had never been a big concern for him personally, but the reality of a small refuge accountable to a board of directors meant he had to worry about things like that on occasion.

As a secretary, Portia was brilliant—organized, dedicated—exactly what a free-spirited guy like him needed. But he also wanted her, as a man, and that made working with Portia increasingly challenging.

Since he'd hired her, he'd noticed her—and then he'd immediately move his attention back to business. But now, he caught himself distracted by the pinkness of her lips, the way she straightened her ponytail when she was thinking. Over and over, he'd replayed that night in his head. In a perfect world, he could have both. His kick-ass secretary and his sexy lover, too. But Portia had made it damn clear he wasn't welcome in her bed again. She'd sent him a brief morning-after text and then ignored his messages unless they were work related.

His heart pounded as he thought of the last—and only—time they'd been together. The memory ramped him up—before he deliberately pushed it aside.

Regaining focus on the present, he surveyed her tight smile. Portia hadn't said much in the past few minutes, but as if she needed to fill the space with words, she sliced through his thoughts. "So do you think the bird broke a wing?"

He blinked, troubled at the formality of her tone. "Perhaps. I'll have to x-ray it to be certain."

"Good. I'm glad we were able to help him." Matter-of-fact as ever. All business. No hint, no trace of anything more.

She pulled the truck into the driveway of the clinic, parking it. As she turned to face him, he saw concern pass through her eyes. Had she been that worried about his fall?

His fingers ached to touch her bare skin, to explore her gentle curves. Although her breasts were more generous than he remembered. What else had he remembered wrong from their dimly lit, rushed lovemaking? The space between them dwindled, electricity sparking in the air there.

Her eyes danced, and he saw that spark take hold in her, too. The same spark from the night of the storm.

He wanted to nurture that spark into a flame.

He kissed her. God, he kissed her. Tried to rein himself in so he could savor the moment rather than risking another fast and furious encounter. He didn't want to send her running as he had before. But damn, she tasted good. Felt good. He slid his hands up to cup her face.

For an incredible moment, she seemed to kiss him back. Then everything shifted. She pulled away, her skin sickly pale.

And then she opened the door and ran. More than ran. She flat-out bolted before he could even form a syllable.

This man had a way of flipping her stomach upside down on a regular day, and now that she was pregnant, her stomach didn't seem to know which way was up.

Her ballet flats slammed, skidded against the ground.

Her stomach rumbled a protesting gurgle, bile rising in the back of her throat.

She ran inside the clinic, through the side entrance and toward her office off the main reception space. She sagged back against the wall, sliding down to the floor while trying to decide if she needed to race the rest of the way to the restroom or simply stay put, calm, unmoving.

Yes, staying still was best. She drew in one deep breath after another. With each breath, she tried to focus on her immediate surroundings. At least the normally bustling clinic lacked people at this hour. All the staff and volunteers had gone home after settling the animals in for the night. Good, she'd hate to have an audience for this. Her eyes adjusted to the dim light, and she heard the creak of the door that lead to the supply closet.

Portia swallowed again, feeling unease and nausea reclaim her stomach.

A light flicked on in an adjoining office with the door open. Maureen. Easton's research assistant and sister-in-law. Like Easton, Maureen put in long hours, sacrificing sleep for the animals' sake.

She had a clipboard in her hand, and a pen tucked in her hair. Maureen must've been doing inventory. While keeping a meticulous inventory made life at the clinic run smoothly during all seasons, hurricane season made this task rise to a new level of importance. If the intensity of the tropical storm a few weeks ago was any indication of the hurricanes to come, Portia knew how vital it would be to the survival of the refuge for them to maintain plans and supplies.

But what of her own plans?

Portia took a steadying breath as Maureen noticed

her and came over. Her bright red hair bouncing in curls, Maureen crouched next to Portia, green eyes searching.

"Are you okay?" Maureen's slight Irish brogue lilted.

"I'm fine. I just forgot to eat dinner and I'm light-headed. Low blood sugar. I'll be fine."

Standing, Maureen opened a drawer in the supply room, the one where she'd stashed other sorts of emergency supplies—saltines, PowerBars and gum. "You work too hard."

Maureen tossed her a packet of crackers. To Portia's surprise, she actually caught the wrapped package, shaking hands and all. Tearing open the wrapper, Portia stood and took her time nibbling while she searched for the right words to deflect Maureen's comment.

"I enjoy my work." Not completely true.

She was grateful for her well-paying job and the adorable one-bedroom cabana that came with it. She had a dream of becoming a teacher one day, but she needed to pay for her brother's education and save enough to finance her own—

Except that wasn't going to happen. She was out of time to fulfill her own dreams. She had to think of her brother and this baby. And even if her pay doubled, there wasn't even enough time to figure all of that out before she had to confess everything to Easton.

She hated thinking about money at all. It made her feel too much like her gold digger mother. But there were practical realities to consider.

Like getting some crackers into her stomach before she hurled.

She nibbled on the edge of a saltine. Each bite settling her stomach. For the moment, anyway.

Maureen glanced around the clinic, leaning around

the corner that lead to the examination room. "Where's the doctor?"

"He's examining an injured bird we rescued." Or so she assumed. She'd left him in a bit of a hurry.

What on earth had he been thinking to kiss her like that?

More to the point, what had she been thinking to allow it to happen? To respond? Normally, she prided herself on her control. Her good sense. With Easton, it seemed, she had neither.

Maureen passed over a container of wet wipes, her bright diamond ring glittering. Recently, she'd married Easton's brother, Xander. "Here."

"What?" Portia took them, confused.

"You've got dust on your knees and on your elbows."

She looked down to check, heat flaming her cheeks as she remembered being close to Easton. Of their bodies pressed against each other on the hard ground. Not that she intended to share those details with anyone. "It's messy work out there."

As if on cue to make her cheeks flame hotter, the side door opened and she heard the long stride that was distinctly Easton's. From a distance, he glanced at her, the bird cradled against his chest in a careful but firm hold.

Maureen stepped forward. "Do you need help?"

He shook his head. "I've got this. You two carry on."

Easton headed toward the back where they did X-rays, away from other animals. His footsteps grew softer until the sound faded altogether.

Maureen turned back to her. "You seem more of the office job type. I've often wondered what made you take on this position." Blunt and honest conversation with Maureen. While normally Portia appreciated Maureen's directness, Portia didn't know if she had the stamina for this sort of exchange right now.

"The pay is more than generous and the locale is enticing."

Did that sound as lame out loud as she thought? Didn't matter. It was true. She'd needed the better-than-average pay, with housing included, to save the money she needed to pay for her brother. Her stomach did another flip and she reached for a cracker. The scents of the clinic were bothering her in a way they normally didn't—the stringent smell of antiseptic cleaner used religiously on every surface, the wood shavings lining crates, the air of live plants.

"And the pay is such because the other secretaries before you couldn't handle an eccentric boss and his unconventional hours, helping him with X-rays, the animals and fieldwork, cleaning his messy office…or they tried to put the moves on him. And yet you've put up with him even though he's clearly not your type."

Portia stiffened, biting down hard on the edge of the cracker. She chewed and swallowed before speaking. "What would my type be?"

"Did I sound presumptuous? I'm sorry if that came out wrong."

"Not at all. I'm truly curious because… Oh, never mind." The question had sounded innocent, but in a strange way, Portia began to wonder if Maureen knew, or at the very least suspected something had happened between Portia and Easton.

"I just meant I can see you with a suave, well-traveled businessman or a brilliant professor. But of course you're clearly more than capable of taking care of your own love life. Tell me about your type? Or maybe there's already a gentleman in your life?"

A gentleman in her life? Time for a stellar deflection.

Portia arched her brow and rolled her eyes. She did everything she could to visually signify that she had no connection to anyone at all. One of Portia's greatest strengths had always been hiding behind conversation.

"Tell me about your honeymoon plans." That topic ought to do it. Maureen and Xander had delayed their honeymoon trip because, after they were married, they'd realized just how deeply they cared for each other. Originally their marriage had been for convenience—he'd needed a wife to keep custody of his daughter and she'd needed citizenship—but it had since deepened into true love.

"I cannot wait, Portia. It will be hard to be away from Rose for two weeks, but she'll be staying with her grandparents."

Rose, Xander's sweet, blonde baby girl. Portia's unborn baby's cousin.

The weight of that sentiment slammed into her every fiber.

Her baby and Rose would be family. Portia's hand settled on her stomach. She was connected to this place and this family now, no matter what.

Portia's brother was connected too, through her, even though he lived in the panhandle—in Pensacola, Florida—getting ready to enter his last year of college. He had emotional support from their aunt nearby, but the older woman barely made ends meet. She had gone above and beyond by taking the two of them in after their mother drank herself into liver failure when Portia was thirteen and her brother, Marshall, was only seven.

It was up to Portia to support her family—including this unexpected baby.

Her head started spinning with how tangled everything had become.

Maureen stepped forward, concern creasing her brow. "Are you sure you're feeling alright?"

"It was a long work day. I'm hungry and exhausted. That's all."

She needed to get herself together. Wear looser clothes if need be. Give herself a chance to verify everything was alright with the pregnancy and if it was, take the time she needed to come up with a plan for her future.

She'd worked too hard for her independence to give it up now, no matter how tempting Easton might be.

Two

What the hell was up with Portia?

When he'd stepped into the wildlife preserve's main building, he had taken note of her pale face and standoffish demeanor. Leaving her alone to talk with Maureen seemed the best option. He'd heard the two women leave a half hour later, each sending a quick farewell shout before heading out.

Easton understood that Portia regretted their impulsive encounter during the tropical storm. He'd almost started to accept that it wouldn't be leading anywhere. It was one night and no more.

But then he'd seen that look in her eyes today.

Shaking his head in bemusement, he closed the clinic door and punched in the security code before turning away into the inky dark. Night creatures spoke to him through the cover of darkness, a cooing mix of coastal birds and tropical bugs. He could identify each sound as readily as he could identify different human voices. As a young boy, Easton digested each sound the way some men committed the sounds of roaring engines to memory. He knew each voice and wanted to help ensure they all continued to speak.

He'd had offers to work at other, larger clinics in more exotic locales, but the newly named Lourdes Family Wildlife Refuge was a personal quest for him and his brother. And he liked this place he called home.

As much as he'd enjoyed his eccentric life growing up, always on the move with his globe-trotting parents, he also enjoyed waking up in the same place each morning. The Key Largo–based animal preserve blended the best of both worlds for him—the wilds and home.

Even the main house reflected that balance of barely domesticated wildness. A sprawling mansion, it stood two stories tall, complete with open balconies and an extravagant, oasis-inspired pool.

Which was where Easton was headed now. His brother, Xander, sat alone on one of the lounge chairs, a glass of bourbon neat in his hand.

Easton and his brother had always been different but close. Since their parents traveled the world with little thought of creating a home or helping their kids build friendships, he and his brother relied on each other. Even more so after their father died and their mother continued her world-traveling ways, always looking for the next adventure in each new country rather than staying in one place to connect with her children.

This house represented more than Easton's commitment to preserving animals in Key Largo. This shared space with his brother represented an attempt at familial cohesion. An attempt at proving they could grow something stable, something to be proud of. The moonlight filtered through stray clouds, peppering his walk in a play of shadow and light on the well-maintained lawn.

He didn't want to blame his parents. They deserved to live their lives as they wanted, to be themselves. And even if they hadn't been conventional parents, they had more than lived up to their commitment to feed, house and educate their children.

But as much as he didn't want to blame them, he'd found his rocky relationship with them had influenced him. He found it difficult to sustain lasting relationships with women. He'd had a series of short romances. And the only time he'd even considered the altar, she— Dana—had split up with him right before he could propose. She'd said he was too eccentric, too much of a kid at heart, for a committed relationship.

Which was ironic as hell since he'd already been looking at engagement rings.

He hadn't told her that. Dana probably would have said he wouldn't have been much of a husband, or that he wouldn't have actually bought a ring. And she probably would have been right. He knew he was eccentric, and he'd worked to find the right career to blend his passion and personality with work he cared about. He got to climb trees and play in the woods for a living. Not too shabby as a way of channeling his strengths. He'd taken what he'd inherited of his parents' quirky ways and toned them down, figuring out how to stay in one place.

None of that seemed to matter, though, when it came to figuring out how to settle down, based on his history with Dana, Laura, Naomi... Damn, he was depressing the hell out of himself.

So where did that leave him with Portia?

Once on the stone ground that surrounded the pool, he grabbed a plush lounge chair and pulled it beside Xander. Easton sat in the middle of the lounger, facing his brother. Xander's ocean-colored eyes flicked to him.

Xander had taken on the wildlife preserve in memory of his wife's passing. Reviving the then struggling refuge had been her passion.

This place meant the world to both brothers.

"What's the deal with you and Portia?" Xander's tone was blunt and businesslike—the commanding voice that won him boardroom battles left and right.

"What do you mean?" The answer came too quickly out of Easton's mouth.

"Don't play dumb with me. I was out for a walk with Rose and I saw the way you looked at Portia when you both got into the truck earlier." He sipped his bourbon, fixing Easton with the stare of an older brother.

"Why didn't you say hello or offer to help out?"

"You're trying to distract me. Not going to work. So what gives between you two?"

Easton chose his words carefully, needing to regain control of the conversation before his brother went on some matchmaking kick that would only backfire by making Portia retreat. She was prickly.

And sexy.

And not going to give him the brush-off another time. She'd been avoiding him more than ever recently and he was determined to find out the reason.

"Easton?" Xander pushed.

"She's an attractive woman." Not a lie.

"A cool woman, classic. And she's been here awhile. She's also not your type. So what changed?"

She absolutely wasn't the sort to go out with a guy

like him. And yet there was chemistry between them. Crackling so tangibly he could swear he was standing in the middle of a storm with the heavens sending lightning bolts through him. She clearly felt the same way, except the next morning, once the storm had passed, she'd insisted it couldn't happen again. He'd thought if he waited patiently she would wear down.

She hadn't.

Until today. "And what would my type be?"

"You really want me to spell that out?" Xander's crooked glance almost riled Easton.

Almost. Then he reminded himself he was the chill brother normally. He was letting this business with Portia mess with his head.

"No need to spell it out. I'll get defensive and have to kick your ass."

"You can try."

Easton smiled tightly. As kids, he used to lie in wait for Xander, always trying to best him in an impromptu wrestling match. He won about half of the time, which wasn't too bad considering his older brother had shot up with height faster and Easton hadn't caught up—and passed him—until they were in high school. Now, they had exchanged the good-natured physical wrestling for well-placed banter.

Silence between the brothers lingered, allowing the chorus of nocturnal creatures to swell. Not that he minded. Easton and Xander could both get lost in their own thoughts, with neither of them rambling on with nonsensical chatter. He'd always appreciated the ability to hang out with his brother without feeling the need to fill every moment with speech.

Easton had to admit Xander was right. Easton had always dated women who were more like him, free-spirited, unconventional types.

Date?

That didn't come close to describing what had happened between him and Portia.

And maybe that was the problem. What had stopped him from asking her out on a date? Before that night, he'd wanted to keep their relationship professional. But after they'd crossed that line… He'd been trying to talk to her about that night. But he'd never done the obvious. Ask her out to dinner…and see where things progressed from there.

He'd always been a man of action and speed. But why not take things slowly with her? He had all the time in the world.

Easton didn't know where things were heading with Portia, but he wasn't giving up. He hoped that dating was the right plan and considered asking Xander for input. Usually he and his brother told each other everything, relied on each other for support—hell, they'd been each other's only friend when they'd been traveling with their parents. Easton needed a plan. And his brother was good at plans, and Xander had far more success in the romance department.

Except right now Easton wanted to hold on to the shift in his relationship with Portia. Keep that private between the two of them. He didn't want to risk word getting out and spooking her.

Because, yes, something had changed between Easton and his brother too since Xander had married Maureen, and Easton couldn't figure out what that was. His brother had been married before and had loved his wife, mourned her deeply when she'd died. Still, Easton hadn't felt he'd lost a part of his brother then, not like now.

So yeah, he wasn't ready to share yet.

Or maybe it had nothing to do with his brother.

And everything to do with Portia.

Up until realizing she was pregnant, the most anxiety-inducing moments in Portia's life had been when she'd fretted about taking care of her brother and paying bills.

This morning had combined all of her anxieties. Her secret pregnancy coupled with arriving to work a half hour late. She'd been sick for what felt like hours and it had thrown her off schedule. Portia was never, ever late. Tardiness drove her insane. Since the morning sickness seemed to be getting significantly worse, she might have to move up her appointment with the doctor to next week. That made her stomach flip all the more since it would mean facing the uncomfortable reality of having to tell Easton.

Dr. Lourdes.

Her boss.

Damn.

Refocus. She pushed those thoughts out of her mind. Easton's schedule needed to be organized for the day. That wouldn't happen if she didn't collect herself right now. Tugging on the sleeves of her light pink cardigan, she stepped into the office, ready to do prep work for Easton's arrival.

Blinking in the harsh white light, her tumultuous stomach sank. Easton sat behind his desk, already at work.

His collar-length dark hair was slicked back, blue eyes

alert and focused on a stack of papers in front of him, full lips tightly pressed as he thought.

She drew in a sharp breath, another wave of nausea and dizziness pressing at her. He looked up from his desk, his clean-shaven face crinkled in a mixture of concern and…surprise? She realized *he* was the one all put together this morning and *she* was the one feeling scattered and disorganized.

This sudden reversal robbed her of her focus. His eyes traced over her, his head falling to the side in concern.

"Are you okay? It's just—you are never late. In fact, you arrive to everything at least fifteen minutes early." He set his pen down, eyes peering into hers.

She swallowed, her throat pressing against the top button of her off-white button-up shirt and her strand of faux pearls. Part of her wanted to lean on him, confide in him and get his support. But how? She didn't have much practice in asking for help.

"Uh." Stammering, her mind blanked. "Yeah. I just… I think I may have the stomach flu. I haven't felt this bad in ages."

She put a hand to her stomach as if to emphasize her symptoms. But really, her palm on her stomach just reminded her of the life growing inside her and how difficult telling Easton was going to be.

"I think that is going around. Maureen called out with the same symptoms. Should you go rest?"

"I'll be fine. I've got crackers and ginger ale on hand. Anyway, how's our little patient doing this morning, Doctor?" She added the last part to keep a professional distance between them.

"Walking around, even attempting to take flight. X-rays show no breaks in the wings and there are no missing feathers, so I'm guessing it's a strained muscle that will benefit from rest. Then back into the wild." He ran his hands through his hair, his athletic build accented with the movement.

"That's good to know. Your risky climb saved his—or her—life."

"His," he answered simply.

Oppressive silence settled between them. She hated this. There had been a time, not even that long ago, where conversation had felt easy and natural between them. But since the tropical storm, she'd looked for every reason to put distance between them. This morning was no different. "If you're busy with patients, then I'll get to some transcriptions."

"Actually, I'm not busy with patients. Let the transcriptions wait." His voice dropped any pretense of nonchalance. Determination entered his tone.

"Okay. But why?"

"Let's talk."

Every atom in her being revolted. Talk? How could she begin to talk to him? She wasn't ready. She needed more time.

"I don't think that's a good idea. We don't talk. We work." She fished the planner out of her oversize bag and waved it in the air.

"I think talking is an excellent idea." A small, hungry smile passed over his lips, blue eyes shining with familiar mischief.

Why did he have to be so damn sexy?

"Please, don't make things more awkward than—"

"Go out with me on a date."

A date? With Dr. Easton Lourdes? The world slammed still. "A what?"

"A date, where two people spend time together at some entertaining venue. Tomorrow's not a workday, so it can be afternoon or evening. I don't want to presume what you would enjoy because honestly, you're right, we haven't spoken very much. So for our date, what do you think about a wine-tasting cruise?"

She couldn't drink, not while pregnant. She winced.

"Okay," Easton said, moving from behind his desk, "from the look on your face I'll take that as a no. Concert in the park with a picnic? Go snorkeling? Or take a drive down to the tip of the Keys and hang out at Hemingway's old house or climb to the top of the Key West Lighthouse?"

"You're serious about wanting to go on a date?" What would she have thought if he'd made that request months ago? Or if she weren't pregnant now? What if he'd made that request when she had the luxury of time to explore the possibility of feelings between them?

Except she didn't have time.

He sat on the edge of his desk, a devilish look in his eyes. "Serious as a heart attack."

She could see by his face he meant it. Totally. He wanted to go on a date with her. She'd spent two years attracted to him while never acting on it in order to maintain her independence and now—when the last thing she should be doing was starting an affair with him—he was asking her out.

Her emotions were clouding her judgment. Their impulsive night of sex had flipped her mind upside down. Their attraction was every bit as combustible as she'd expected. It had stolen her breath, her sanity. She'd even entertained pursuing something with him. For a moment, she'd not cared one whit about her independence. But fears had assailed her the next morning. Heaven knew if he'd suggested a date then, she would have run screaming into the Everglades, never to be seen again.

Okay, maybe that was overstating things. Or maybe not.

But it did bring up the point that now, things were different. She really did need to talk to him soon and come up with a plan for their baby. Meanwhile, though, maybe she could use this time to get to know him better on a friendship level and find the best way to tell him about their "love child."

She just had to ignore the electricity that sizzled between them every time he looked at her.

"Key West," she said. "Let's take the drive to see Hemingway's house."

The romantic ride he'd planned just yesterday to Hemingway's house had somehow gone awry.

What should have been a leisurely scenic drive down the heart of the Florida Keys was getting him nowhere with Portia. He wanted her to open up to him, to reveal something about herself. But she was totally clammed up and he was on fire to know more about her. To find a way past her defenses and back into her bed. To pull her clothes off, slowly, one piece at a time and make love to her in a bed, at a leisurely pace rather than a frenzied coupling in a bathroom during a storm.

And she'd gone into her Ice Queen mode again.

Which had never overly bothered him before but was, for some reason, making him crazy now. Yes, he burned to know more about her than what she took in her coffee—although these days she seemed to enjoy water with fruit slices more than her standard brew. He needed to get her talking.

And he also needed to power his way past this slower moving traffic into a clearer stretch of road.

Checking the rearview mirror, he slid his vintage Corvette into the fast lane, getting out from behind a brake-happy minivan. As they passed the van, he noted the map sprawled out on the dash. That explained everything about the somewhat erratic driving behavior.

He used the opportunity of an open road to check out Portia, noting her slender face, porcelain skin and pointed nose. The edges of her mouth were tensed slightly. Her hair was gathered into a loose ponytail, not completely down, but definitely more casual than her usual tightly pulled-back twist. The hairstyle had led him to believe getting through to her today would be easier.

Apparently, he would have to work harder at getting her to reveal her thoughts. And work harder at restraining the urge to slide his hands through her hair until it all hung loose and flowing around her shoulders. He remembered well the feel of those silken strands gliding through his fingers as he moved inside her—

Hell, there went his concentration again.

He draped his wrist over the steering wheel and searched for just the right way to approach her. Often times the simplest ways worked best. Maybe he'd been trying too hard.

"When my brother and I were kids traveling the world with our parents, we became masters at entertaining ourselves during long flights. I'm thinking now might be a good time to resurrect one of our games."

She tipped her head toward him. "Oh really? What did you two play?"

Ah, good. She'd taken the bait.

"Our favorite was one we called Quiz Show. I was about ten when we started playing. I was determined to beat my older brother at something. He was still so much taller, but I figured since we were just a year apart, I had a fighting chance at taking him down in a battle of the minds."

"Tell me more," she said, toying with the end of her ponytail, which sent his pulse spiking again.

"We'd already been on a transcontinental flight and then had to spend ten more hours in a car. So we'd burned out on books and toys and homework. We started asking each other outrageous questions to stump each other."

The result? Two very tight brothers. He hoped to re-create that experience with Portia. To learn something about her. "Would you like to play?"

"Uh, sure. You go first, though, and I reserve the right not to answer."

"Fair enough." A natural quizmaster, he paused, thinking of his first question. One that would help them flow into more personal topics. "What do you do for fun?"

"Are you being rude?" she asked indignantly.

Well, hell. "What do you mean?"

"You said the questions were meant to stump the other person so your question could be taken as an insult."

"Damn. I didn't mean that at all. How about consider this as a new game, our rules. I meant what does Portia oto do for fun? To unwind? Because I don't know you well and I'm trying to get to know you better." He needed more than just raw data. He wanted her quirks, her idiosyncrasies. He wanted to figure out his attraction to her. Once he did, then he could put those tumultuous dreams to rest.

Or know whether to pursue an all-out affair.

She shot him a sideways look, her ponytail swishing, the ribbon rippling in the wind. "Okay, I see what you mean. But you have to promise not to laugh at my answer."

"I would never. Unless you tell me you make to-do lists for fun. Then I might." He kept his tone casual, his grip on the leather steering wheel light.

"I may be a Post-it note princess, but that isn't my 'fun' time. No. I actually like to draw." She said the words so quietly that they were almost swept away by the wind.

"You draw?" He spared her a sidelong glance, noting the way her cheeks flushed, even beneath her oversize sunglasses.

She nodded, pony tail bobbing. "I do."

"Well, what do you like to draw?" He pressed for progress.

She took a deep breath, hand floating in the air as she made an uncharacteristically theatrical gesture that drew his attention to her elegant fingers. "Oh, you know, the usual kinds of things. Animals mostly. Lots of animals. People, too. Their faces especially. I like the small details."

"You are just full of surprises, Ms. Soto." He bet her way of noticing made her a brilliant artist. Nothing seemed to escape her gaze. He liked that about her. He was finding he liked a lot more about her than he'd realized. Apparently before now his absentminded professor ways had made him miss things. His attention to detail wasn't as fine-tuned as hers.

Something he intended to rectify.

"Hmm. I can be... Well, how about you, *Doctor* Lourdes? What do you do for fun?"

His formal salutation felt unnatural coming from her. He knew she used it to put distance between them, but he wasn't allowing it this time. "I'm afraid to confess my favorite downtime activity is fishing."

"Really?"

In the corner of his vision, he saw her angle toward him.

"Really," he responded without hesitation. "I know some would say that goes against the conservationist, animal lifesaving oath I took, but I'm not a vegetarian and I always eat what I catch."

"It's not bungee jumping or something equally adrenaline inducing?"

"I know. I'm a letdown. I like fishing because I enjoy the quiet time to think and reflect. And I'm humbled by the way the ecosystem works—how connected everything is."

"Now who is full of surprises?" she murmured, more to herself than to him.

"My turn. What about your dreams? What do you really want to do?"

"I'm happy to be your assistant."

He shook his head. "Not what I asked."

They were only a few minutes away from the Hemingway Home and Museum, and the traffic around them increased, taillights glowing all around like a faux fire.

Portia tugged on her ponytail, thinking.

"In a perfect world? Like a money-and-responsibility-free world?"

"Yep." Tall palms stretched above them, casting shadows over her face.

The bright-colored houses and tropical foliage made the island look more like a movie set than reality. Foot traffic was dense too, but the cruise ship passengers on tour for the day would be pulling out before too long and things would quiet down.

"I think I'd like to do something with art. Maybe a nonprofit for kids that focused on creativity after school. Especially for kids who don't have a strong family support system. I'd love to help them see they have the ability to create something beautiful and wonderful."

Her words touched him as he turned the corner, traffic heavier as they drew closer to the historic landmark. "That's a wonderful idea. There isn't enough of that in the world. Any particular reason you chose this need over others?"

"When I was younger, I saw a lot of kids bogged down by circumstances out of their control and they had no outlets of support. I hated that."

He could hear in her voice a more personal reason for her dream, one he felt like she wanted to share. This woman was more like the one he remembered from the night of the storm, the Portia who'd told him of her need to keep on the lights during storms as a child so her brother and her stuffed animals wouldn't be afraid. But he'd seen in her eyes that she'd craved that light and comfort then too, but even now was unwilling to admit her own need for support. Even as her standoffish ways frustrated him at times, he also couldn't help but admire her strength.

If he could keep her talking, he could win her over. What he'd do once he had her, he wasn't sure. All he knew was that he wanted her like he'd wanted no one and nothing else.

But how to tease this information out of her?

He slowed the car to a halt, the traffic in front of him growing worse.

And then the unthinkable happened, interrupting his thoughts. A crash echoed in his ears less than an instant before the car jolted forward.

They'd been rear-ended. Damn. His protective instincts went on high alert and his arm shot across in front of Portia.

Only keeping her safe mattered.

Three

Her near-electric moment with Easton ended with a re-sounding thud.

A minivan had rear-ended them.

Easton had flung his right arm out to protect her… and protect their unborn child. Not that he knew anything about the baby, and she wasn't any closer to being ready to tell him on this far-from-normal day.

As far as dates went, her romantic outing with Easton had been anything but typical. Yet not in the quirky up-for-whatever way that normally characterized Easton's gestures. She'd seen his protective impulses around his niece and the animals. But this was the first time Portia had been on the receiving end. If she weren't stunned—and more than a little afraid—she would think longer on how that made her feel.

His blue eyes filled with concern as his hand reached for hers, helping her step out of the car.

"I'll be fine." She waved him off, eager to get out of the Corvette and take dozens of deep breaths away from the scent of scorched rubber and brakes. "I promise, I will tell you if I feel the least need to go to the doctor."

And she would. Keeping her secret wasn't worth risking her child. Already, she could hear sirens and see cop cars, firetrucks and an EMT vehicle. She would check in with a medical tech.

"All right. I'll go give the statement to the police." He squeezed her hand quickly before walking away to check in with one of the officers.

One deep breath after another, she calmed her nerves, taking comfort in the strong breadth of Easton's shoulders. She winged a prayer of thanksgiving that he was okay, as well. This could have been so much worse than a dented fender.

In all honesty, she had been in a worse accident when she was thirteen, shortly before her mom died. Her mother had taken her to school in a little blue car. At the final turn before the school, they'd been sideswiped by a bright red pickup truck. That day, she'd needed stitches, and her mother had severely damaged her already ravaged liver. Only a few months later, her mother had died, leaving Portia and her brother alone. They'd moved from Nevada and into the house with their father's older sister in Florida.

While today's crash had only been a fender bender and there were no overt signs of damage, still, she worried. Had the crash harmed her unborn baby?

The thought brought a wave of nausea as the steady swirl of red-and-blue lights echoed in Portia's peripheral vision. How much longer until those emergency vehicles wove their way closer?

She was responsible for the life growing inside her. The life she had to protect. A little boy or little girl—

And thank goodness, one of the EMS trucks stopped on the shoulder of the road just one car up. Since there wasn't a line of others who appeared in need of emergency care, she pushed away from the light pole and moved toward the ambulance.

Smoothing her sundress in an excuse to steady her hands, she approached the younger of the two EMTs. The gold name tag read Valez.

"Uh, sir?" Stammering, she twisted her fingers together, a flush crawling across her face.

"Yes, ma'am?" Valez, a man in his midthirties with a jet-black mustache, asked, gesturing toward the back of the ambulance.

"I feel fine. But…" Oh Lord. This was the first time she would talk about her pregnancy out loud. "I'm pregnant and I just want to make sure everything is alright." The rest of the sentence flew out of her mouth, the reality of her situation echoing back to her.

"You did the right thing in coming over here, ma'am. Please, sit down. We'll get you checked out. If you need additional care, we'll transport you to the nearest hospital. But let's hope that's not needed. Okay?" He lifted her wrist and began taking her pulse. "So just relax and let's talk. How far along are you?" He glanced at her while waving a hand for the other EMT to come over. The older gentleman handed Valez a bag filled with equipment.

"Umm. Well, not quite two months. But fairly close to that point." Portia's voice was a whisper, nearly covered by the sounds of car horns and conversations.

Valez's brow furrowed, reaching for his stethoscope. "And so far, your pregnancy is going well?"

"Yes."

He checked her pulse, nodding to her. "So far, your vitals seem just fine."

Deep breath out. Good. "What should I watch for?"

Handing his equipment back to the other EMT, Valez turned to face her. "There are two things you can watch for—bleeding and cramping. Based on your vitals, I think you are in the clear. Just be sure to put your feet up and try to relax."

Portia's vigorous nod sent loose tendrils of her hair out of her ponytail and into her face. Before she could respond to Valez, Easton strode toward them, concern wearing lines in his ruggedly handsome face.

"Everything okay?"

Heart palpitating, palms sweating, she urged her tongue to find words. "Fine, I'm just fine."

He glanced at the EMT. "Is that true? She's a tough cookie who doesn't complain."

Valez nodded, holding his medical kit. "We've checked her over and everything appears fine. She knows what signs to look for."

"Signs to look for?" Easton's brow furrowed, looking confused.

Damn.

Panic pulsed in her throat. This could not be how he found out.

The two technicians exchanged glances. Valez cleared his throat. "Yes, symptoms to look for after a car accident."

"Symptoms?"

She tried to interrupt, panicked over what the tech might give away, but he nodded at her reassuringly.

"Whiplash, for example. If your neck feels stiff in the

morning. Or aches from the seatbelt or from the impact if your airbag went off."

She inched away. "No airbag. Our vehicle was barely tapped, but I appreciate all the other information you provided. Truly." She spun to Easton. "We should clear out so they can check out any others who need help."

"Okay," Easton answered, giving a final wave to the EMT. "Thank you for taking the time to be so thorough. I appreciate it."

"Just doing our job." The tech nodded to her. "Take it easy, ma'am."

Easton turned back to her, gesturing to the slightly damaged car. A deep sigh escaped his lips, though when he turned to face Portia, a smile manifested. An easygoing smile. One she wanted to give in to. She wanted to lean on him, to rely on him, but she knew that was a recipe for disaster. She had to do this on her own. The sensible thing? Cut her losses on today—on the idea of them.

He touched the top of her arm with gentle fingertips. "This is not the way I envisioned our date going, but I'm glad no one was injured. You must be starving. I know I am. Would you like indoor or outdoor dining?"

The accident shook her ability to remain calm. Though her vitals checked out, she worried about the baby. And that worry made her realize the futility of pursuing anything personal or romantic with Easton. She would always be connected to him, but she couldn't come to rely on him.

"Honestly, I would like to pick up to-go food and head home."

"I know it's a long day driving the whole way down the Keys. Would you rather we get a hotel?" he asked, rushing to add, "Separate rooms of course, if that's what you want."

"I want to go home."

Portia felt downright foolish. She needed space—a place to think. Somewhere away from Easton.

He studied her eyes for a long moment, then shrugged, "Sure, your day. Your date. But it's going to be damn good carryout."

Thoughts of the accident still shook Easton. Though small, the fender bender replayed in his mind.

Portia's scrunched brow visibly displayed her stress. Her demeanor shifted after talking to the EMT. Easton had the sinking feeling that she wasn't as fine as she let on. Or maybe the accident had spooked her as it had spooked him. She'd been initially hesitant to accept his offer of the date. Maybe she'd interpreted the accident as a sign that they had to turn back.

He fished his soda out of the cup holder and sipped on the cola. She was safe. They were both safe. The car had received some damage, but that didn't matter. Not really.

Portia, currently chowing down on carryout, appeared pale, but her color was returning by the bite. She'd chosen a hogfish sandwich, which he hadn't expected at all, even though the delicate fish had a scallop flavor he personally enjoyed. But he'd thought she would order something grilled on top of a salad, the kind of thing she'd pick up locally when she grabbed them takeout for lunch if she needed to go into town on a workday. Yet, this time she'd chosen heartier fare and downed the sandwich like a starved woman. Even alternating each bite with a conch fritter.

This glimpse of her zest for life, her savoring of the

senses, made him hungry for a taste of her. He'd wanted to stop for a roadside picnic, but she'd shot down the suggestion, noting the gathering storm clouds. He had to concur. They needed to start for home.

Traffic in the northbound lane moved moderately fast, but allowed Easton to take in the scenery. Sometimes, he felt like he lived at the refuge. Not a big complaint—he loved his work, knew caring for the animals transcended a job and landed squarely in the realm of a vocation. But he often forgot what a normal day looked like.

Then again, his unconventional childhood had never really allowed for normalcy either.

Regardless, the drive reminded him of just how damn lucky he was to live in the tropical Florida Keys. People on bikes lined sidewalks. Palm trees bowed in the summer wind. Easton could make out the turquoise of the sea catching radiantly in the sunlight, the shoreline dotted with shacks that were homes and shops, colorful and scenic. The natural panoramic view was gorgeous.

But not nearly as gorgeous as the woman next to him.

Portia continued to surprise him. Intrigue him. He had a few hours until they'd be back at the refuge. Maybe he could restart their quiz game. Figure out more about her. Easton wanted to tease answers from her lips. Understand more. He could ask her about her family. He knew nothing about them. In fact, Easton didn't really know much concerning her life before she came to work for him.

He could ask her if she'd ever been close to marriage. Did she want a family of her own? What was the worst kiss she'd ever had? That could at least break the ice and make them laugh. Or he could ask why she'd been avoid-

ing him over the last few weeks when they worked together every day, for crying out loud.

With a renewed commitment to demystifying Portia
Soto, he turned his head, ready to begin the questions
again.

But as he opened his mouth, he knew he couldn't continue.

Her head rested against the window, her eyes were
closed and she was fast asleep. He picked up her empty
food container, tossed it into the carryout bag, and decided to take comfort in the fact that she felt at ease
enough to nap around him. He reached for the radio to
turn on a news channel just as his phone rang, the Blue-
tooth kicking in automatically.

He reached to pick up fast before the tone woke her.
But she only twitched once before settling back into even-
paced breathing.

He spared a quick glance to the caller ID. His brother,
Xander, was on the line. Easton tapped the monitor and
his brother's voice filled the air.

"Hey, dude, check this out." Background noise echoed
as he said, "Rose, baby girl, come back to Daddy and
talk on the phone. Tell Uncle Easton what you just told
Daddy."

Easton's mouth twitched. His brother was such a
devoted father, and it was funny as hell watching his
starched-suit, executive brother wrapped around that tiny
little finger.

Easton's toddler niece babbled for a few indistinguish-
able sentences before she said, "Birdies, birdies."

"That's great, Rosebud." Yeah, Easton had to admit
his niece was mighty damn cute. "Give the phone back
to your daddy now. Love you, kiddo."

"Hey, brother," Xander's voice came back over. "That's awesome, isn't it? We have the next generation of veterinarians in our family."

"Could be, could be." His eyes flicked back to Portia. She readjusted in her seat, sleep still heavy on her brow. The warmth of the afternoon sun hit her cheekbones, making her glow with natural, sexy beauty.

Xander's baritone voice snapped Easton back into focus. "Maybe she'll add to the family portfolio with inventions the way you have."

"She'll one-up me, for sure. And how the hell did you know about that? It was supposed to be—"

Xander cut him off, a smile present in his tone. "A secret and you just invested well, I know. But one of your colleagues saw me at a wildlife preserve convention and thought I was you."

"Ouch." While the brothers shared the same deep blue eyes and broad-chested build, Xander's clean-cut executive look could never be confused with Easton's collar-length hair and slightly disheveled persona.

"It was a windy day. I didn't look like I'd combed my hair."

"I think I was just insulted."

"You were." A laugh rumbled in Xander's throat.

"Thanks."

"No problem. How's it going on your…what was it you were doing today?"

He was probing. Easton could hear it in his voice. Through clenched teeth Easton replied, "A professional run with my assistant."

"Right." Doubt dripped from Xander's tone. Easton could practically see Xander's eyebrow raise, incredulous as always. "How's that going?"

"We'll be back by the end of the day."

"Given your wanderlust soul, something makes me doubt that," Xander teased, but the joke missed its mark. Struck a nerve in Easton.

"We will be."

"That reminds me of when Mom used to say she'd have us all back to the hotel by dinner, but instead, we'd spend the night somewhere unexpected. You've got her sense of time, you know."

Easton's jaw clenched tighter. "See you in a few hours, brother."

He hung up the phone, eyes intensely focused on the road. Wanderlust was one thing, but he still struggled to be taken seriously. To prove he could stay in one spot for a long time, be dedicated to something outside himself. That he wasn't wandering aimlessly in Neverland.

"Easton," Portia's voice jolted him out of his fog. "What did he mean by invention?"

"Oh—" he shrugged "—it's nothing."

"Clearly, it's something—" she paused to sit upright again "—if it added to your family's financial portfolio." She held up a hand. "Wait. Forget I said that."

"Why? I encouraged questions today. Quiz Show, remember? The more outrageous the better."

"Most people find it rude to ask about another person's finances."

"That's not really a secret. And as for my invention…" He shot her a sidelong glance, trying to get a read on her. Truthfully, he felt exposed, talking about this aspect of his work. This idea felt more personal than any bank balance. "It's…I created a shunt to go into the liver duct. It opens and closes in a way that enables multiple testing of a sick animal without multiple sticks."

A smile warmed her face, nose crinkling. "That's really amazing and compassionate."

Eyes back on the road. He changed lanes, sunlight streaming into the car. "The animals I take care of, they're my kids."

"Until you have children of your own."

He shook his head. "I'm not going to have them."

"But you're so great with Rose, I never would have guessed you don't like kids." Shock entered her tone, and Portia cocked her head to the side.

"I do like them. I just don't plan to have any of my own. I'm crummy father material. Too devoted to the job. I expected you of all people to understand that."

She smiled quickly, fidgeting. What had he said wrong?

"You do work long hours," she said simply.

He needed to get this conversation back on track. Heat filled him as he remembered his reason for this little outing in the first place—to romance her—to woo her. To get her back into his bed. "We have spent many, many hours together."

And he hoped to spend many more in a nonbusiness capacity, sooner rather than later. In fact, there was no moment like the present. The accident left him wanting to seize the day. Talk of the invention nudged him to take things in a new direction with Portia.

He eased the vintage car over to the shoulder of the road and turned off the car.

Portia looked around, confused. "What are you doing? Is something wrong with the Corvette?" She fished in her purse and pulled out her phone. "I'll look up the number for auto service—"

"Portia?" He started to lean toward her.

"Yes," she answered without looking up from her phone.

"Stop talking." He cupped her face in his hands and pressed his mouth to hers.

Four

The taste of Easton tantalized her senses, intoxicating and arousing. This was what she'd been trying to forget from their passionate encounter the night of the tropical storm. A night she hadn't spoken of since then, except in vague references, but a night that had filled her dreams more often than not.

His hand palmed her back and drew her closer until they were chest to chest. Her swollen breasts were especially sensitive and felt the contact all the more acutely. With a will of their own, her fingers crawled up his hard muscled arms to grip his wide shoulders. She wriggled to get closer, her mouth opening wider to take the bold sweep and thrust of his tongue.

Warping her away from reality, the kiss unlocked Portia, electric sensations enlivening her awareness. Her normal laundry list of concerns were rinsed from her mind. Instead, she solely focused on the curve of his lips, his deepening kiss, the sweep of his tongue and the stroke of his hands. He pulled her closer, lifting her out of her seat and into his lap. Holding her in his broad arms, the scent of his amber aftershave mixing with faint sounds of ocean waves crashing to shore. Her fingers wandered into his long hair, silky beneath them and she relished every moment of making an even bigger mess of his normally tousled mane.

She'd slept with him—albeit a hurried encounter. Still, she knew the full extent of his appeal, and so she couldn't figure out why a simple kiss could turn her so inside out. Okay, not a simple kiss because nothing with Easton was ever uncomplicated.

Still, she knew the risks of getting too emotionally involved, of depending too heavily on a man. How could her body betray her so, especially after what he'd said about not wanting children? As quickly as that thought hit her she shut it down again. She'd ached to be in his arms again for so long she was a total puddle of hormones in need of an outlet.

In need of *him*.

Now.

His lips moved from her mouth to her jawline to her neck, until her head fell back to give him unfettered access as she reveled in his hungered frenzy. Back resting against the steering wheel, she slipped slightly, the car horn wailing into the moment. Snapping her into the present. Back to the fact that they were on the side of the road and not anywhere private enough for the thoughts shooting through her mind.

As the car horn died, they both winced, a laugh emerging from Easton. He brought his hands to his face, running them through his dark thick hair. Returning to her seat, she laughed too, watching the way his hair fell back into a sexy disheveled mess.

A smile still playing on his lips, he clicked the keys into place, engine warming back up. He steered the yellow Corvette back onto the road, and she settled deeper into the plush leather seat, warmed by their shared exchange of heated breath and hotter skin even as her worries returned.

A calm silence descended, broken only by the slight rustle of tires on gradient pavement.

An unquenchable need to understand what had just happened loosed her lips. "What made you do that?"

Bright blue eyes met hers briefly before he returned his attention to the road. "Because we're dating and you look incredible and I couldn't help myself."

"Dating? This is one date. That's all I agreed to, in case you've forgotten." She felt the need to clarify, because the thought of more scared her. She couldn't risk sliding into an emotional commitment of any kind, not with her and her brother's future so uncertain, not with the secret still looming between her and Easton. This was about getting a sense of him for her child's sake. Wasn't it? Her baby had to come first.

"One date? For today. If I'm not mistaken, you enjoyed that kiss as much as I did. Deny it. I dare you."

"What is this? High school? I'm not taking a dare."

He reached for her hand, the simple gesture sending pulses of interest through her body. Her stomach flipped, phantom traces of his lips echoing along her warming skin.

Easton brought her hand to his lips, the five-o'clock shadow scratching her hand. Teasing. "Double dog dare you."

She choked on a laugh, but kept her hand in his. "That is so...silly."

"Yes, but you're smiling. That's as dazzling as kissing you." He winked and grinned. "And make no mistake, kissing you, just looking at you, is mighty damn amazing." His grin broadened.

And stole her breath.

Her guard was slipping too fast. He was clearly trying to draw her out, and he was succeeding. She needed to erect some boundaries. Fast.

"You can be too charming for your own good sometimes." Her grumble was only halfhearted, she knew. She turned to stare out her window at the dark plumes of violet-gray clouds in the distance. Chances were they would blow northward, but the unpredictability of storms in this state still made her nervous.

"You say that as if it's bad. I'm simply being honest with you."

"How about hush up and drive so we can enjoy the sunset." Tugging her hand from his grasp, Portia leaned forward, watching the sun sink behind the whitecap crests. Easton's declarations rocked her defenses and struck a nerve in her tender heart.

"Can do."

The deep, dark clouds descended on the horizon, hungrily devouring the serenity of the sunset. Rain dripped onto the roof of the Corvette, faster and faster until the drops turned into a violent barrage of water.

So much for that picture-perfect sunset.

* * *

The bad turn in the weather had literally and figura-tively reduced their momentum.

Easton gripped the Corvette's steering wheel in tight hands. For the past two hours, the wall of tropical rain had brought traffic to a crawl. Red brake lights filled the road, their colors seeming to smear as the windshield wipers worked as a frenzied metronome.

While this rain didn't mount to tropical storm level, it was bad enough to back up traffic as people navigated slowly along the packed, narrow road. Many had just pulled off to the side. So many, in fact, the shoulder was lined with vehicles as tightly as the highway.

Whatever electric moment that passed between them had fizzled, fading with each pelt of the rain.

That could be due to the intensity of the storm. Portia's eyes seemed heavy with inexplicable worry.

From beneath his fingertips, he felt a tug on the low-slung Corvette's steering wheel. A result of the piling rain and flooding streets. The tug shifted them slightly to the right, toward the shoulder of the road.

Portia's hand touched his arm, a gesture of reassur-ance. Her lilting voice contrasted against the harsh thun-der. "This is almost as bad as the storm we drove in to rescue the Key deer that had been hit by a car."

He nodded, remembering well that night and how dif-ficult it had been not to kiss away the tenderhearted tears she'd cried. Only the reminder that she was his secretary had kept him from acting on the moonlit impulse. "By the way, this rain is piling up and tugging on the steering—I think it might be slightly worse than the night with the Key deer."

"So more like the time we were transporting the pelican back from Pigeon Key?"

Ah, he recalled that vividly too, how her hair had lifted with the crackle of electricity from the lightning, how his fingers had ached to stroke over the wispy, flyaway strands, how he had realized he was feeling more and more drawn to her the longer they worked together.

So many experiences, long work nights, storms, had been shared between them. And now, another storm and more experiences brewed and crackled. The night she refused to address. That seemed to echo louder than the thunder.

"I'd say so. I mean, just look outside the window, Portia. The water is building on the streets. I think a flood is imminent."

She peered out her window, lips pursing together. As lightening flashed in front of them, he recalled how electric their connection had been during the last tropical storm. The undeniable chemistry had sent them slinking into the bathroom together.

He wanted to touch her like that again. To taste her. But his thoughts were interrupted by the extreme deluge. He could barely see the taillights in front of him.

He had driven in worse when he had to, but right now he didn't have to. They didn't have to. It was more important to be safe.

After the accident earlier today, he wasn't taking any chances. He blipped on the turn signal, seeking shelter on the side of the road.

She turned to him quickly, her lush brown ponytail bouncing, her eyebrows raised. "What are you doing?"

"Pulling over. This is insane to keep driving." He didn't risk taking his eyes off the road as he steered into a tourist shop parking lot with dozens of other cars. "Any problems with that?"

"You're right. No need to risk us getting in another wreck. There are plenty of people who can take care of the animals."

"Maureen is definitely capable." He pulled into an open spot and parked the car.

"Then let's stop for the night." She leaned forward to pick up her purse from the floorboards. "I'll start searching on my phone for a hotel."

"You have to know our chances of finding two rooms open are slim to none."

"I realize that." She pulled out her cell, smiling smartly. "Luckily, you're going to be fine with sleeping on the sofa."

A tapestry of blues and oceanic greens flooded Portia's vision when the door to the honeymoon suite—the only room available on such short notice—swung open.

The Sheltered Crescent Inn sat twenty feet from the ocean, providing panoramic views of the storm. Flashes of pure white light made shadows dance across the room, revealing an array of coastal-themed decorations. Entering the room, a smile lifted Portia's lips. The decorator seemed to have stuffed every free space with conch shells, sailboats and kitchy sayings about life being better at the beach.

Shuffling over a kelp-green rug, she leaned against the solid tan couch, eyes drifting to the open door that led to a luxury bathroom, complete with a spa Jacuzzi built for two.

Fresh-cut roses stood tall in a white vase on the driftwood coffee table. This, of course, was the most expensive room in the inn, and part of her felt bad about having to stay the night here, even though she knew money was no object for him.

The other part of her desired this extra time with Easton. As if by staying in such close proximity, she'd figure out the right words to say to deliver her life-altering news.

Turning her head, she surveyed his broad shoulders, the way his dark hair curled slightly. Ruggedly handsome with those bright blue eyes. His appeal, she tried to tell herself, had not motivated her decision to stay the night with him.

A quick scan revealed a single king-size bed peeking out from the bedroom. But there was no second bed. Just the tan couch she leaned against.

Easton's voice rumbled, and she caught the scent of his spiced cologne as he moved past her to the minibar. "Can I get you something to drink? A snack?"

"Just water for me, please." She pulled her tablet from her purse, the fading, rain-drenched sun just barely reflecting off the screen. "We could work. I have my phone and tablet."

"Do you carry that with you everywhere?" he asked as he poured bottled water into two crystal goblets.

"It's a part of my life," she answered defensively. "Organization is crucial."

"Why?"

"What do you mean by that? It's a positive trait." Frowning, she tugged her ponytail tighter into the scrunchie. She'd been responsible for taking care of her brother when they lived with their mother and she'd found early on that it helped to make lists, to have everything laid out ahead of time, to leave as little as possible to chance.

The crashing of waves echoed in the room blending with the *tap-tap-tap* of the smoldering storm. The deep sounds of thunder ebbed, becoming more and more distant.

He passed her drink to her, their fingers brushing, static snapping like the lightning outside. "Crucial, though? Do you really believe it's that important to be so regimented?"

"Of course I do. It's why you hired me." She caught sight of her own reflection in the glass window. Her hair now perfectly coiffed in a ponytail, but her face bore the stamp of exhaustion she felt tugging at her more and more at the end of each day. "Why are you pushing the point now?"

"Because I can't figure you out."

"Well, the feeling is entirely mutual."

"How so? I'm an open book."

Sort of. And then not at all. "When I took this job, I expected a scientist would be more…scientific."

He clapped a hand to his broad chest. "Have I ever been anything other than effective at work?"

"It's not that. I just didn't expect such a free spirit. Someone who doesn't own a comb and climbs trees." She couldn't hold back her teasing smile even as she knew she was playing with fire by flirting with him.

"I own a comb."

"Do you use it?" She crossed her arms, unable to resist teasing him.

He smiled crookedly, lines of amusement fanning from his eyes into his tanned face.

She nodded. "That's what I thought."

He moved toward the radio, abandoning the work space. She moved past him, his body gently skirting hers, teasing her senses and awareness. Portia's eyes narrowed, suspicious as she sat.

She had to carefully construct her walls, to keep him out of her mind. It would be easy—far too easy—to become undone by his gaze. "Easton…"

"What? We need to listen for weather alerts." He stepped away from the radio. "And I don't need a comb to organize my thoughts. As for organizing everything else, that's what I hire you for. You're stellar at your job, by the way, and I appreciate that more than I can say. I don't want to lose you over…this," he said, waving his hand between them, "either, so I've been taking things slow. But when I saw the look in your eyes after I fell out of that tree, I knew the waiting was over." The corner of his mouth pulled upward, a cocky smile in place. He looked at her hungrily.

"Oh really? This whole romance deal has been because in a weak moment I was actually worried about you?" She'd had no idea she was so transparent.

To him at least.

"Worried? I saw more than concern when you looked at me." His sidelong glance unsettled her.

And made her skin tingle with awareness.

"Easton, is that ego heavy to carry around?"

She tossed a sofa pillow at him. He easily deflected it with an arm.

"Fair enough. Does it help if I say I'm incredibly attracted to you? Because I am." He closed the distance between them, leaning on the other side of the couch. "You don't believe me?"

"I do—you're just…over the top."

"I'm honest. Is that so difficult to believe?" He touched her chin and guided her face toward his. "You're a beautiful woman. So lithe and elegant."

Rain continued to drum on the roof, a soothing sound. But his words gnawed at her. The tone was direct, straightforward, when normally he flirted. So his honest question tugged at her more, compelling her to answer straightforwardly.

"I'm comfortable in my skin, with my life, with my appearance." She brushed off his compliments, the image of her mother manifesting in her mind's eye. "I'm pleased with who I am, and where I'm going in my life."

"And well you should be."

"Thank you." She avoided his gaze, picking up another decorative pillow and hugging this one to her stomach. "That peace was hard-won though."

"How so?" He sat next to her, confusion coating his tone.

His thigh brushed against hers and a part of her wanted to just succumb to the attraction, to avoid this discussion, to avoid the future. But his eyes probed her with undeniable curiosity.

She didn't really like discussing this. Usually made it a habit to avoid this kind of conversation. But she'd decided to share more with him, and she intended to follow through on that. "My mother was the first runner up in the Miss Nevada pageant. She was bombshell gorgeous with pinup poster curves. She'd grown up poor, making her own dresses and costumes. She found her stiletto heels for competitions at yard sales and dyed them herself. The world thought she made a fabulous match with a wealthy casino magnate in Las Vegas, my dad."

Fabulous? More like financial. Her parents had made

each other miserable the minute his money dried up and he'd been sent to prison for tax evasion.

"But you may already know this," she added.

"I don't."

That came as a shock. She would have expected him to know all about her history. "You didn't have me investigated when you hired me? I would think given your family's money..."

"I did a work history check, and called your professional references, all of whom spoke of you in glowing terms. But we're not talking about work. And even if they'd told me personal details, that wouldn't have been from your perspective. I want to hear about your life. From you." His tone was genuine, but firm.

She wasn't used to being the center of attention, and she wasn't sure how she felt about it. But best to finish the story and get the sad truth about it out there and hope he wasn't the sort to judge her for her parents' actions the way others had.

Easton didn't seem the judgmental sort. She liked that about him.

She continued, "My father lost all his money when he went to jail for tax evasion. He died in jail a few months later of some strain of flu—he was a lot older than my mother."

Her dad had kids from another marriage and hadn't been much for the family scene. But he'd taken Portia to work and let her sort casino chips by color. God, she hadn't thought about that ritual of theirs until now.

She shook off the memory and moved on, eager to finish this convoluted history. "My mom...she drank herself into a liver crisis that was compounded by an injury in a car wreck. She died when I was thirteen and my brother was seven."

Portia had been crushed over her father's conviction, and she'd been devastated all over again when she realized her mother had only married for money. Taking the job working for Easton, Portia had been determined not to be drawn in by the wealth of the estate—or the man. And she'd managed to keep her distance from him for nearly two years, only to have her resolve crumble in one emotional night.

"I'm so sorry you had to lose your parents that way."

"Me, too." She shuddered, the memory wounding her all over again. "But they made their choices and paid a high price for them. My brother and I were lucky we had an aunt here in Florida who took us in so we didn't end up in the foster care system."

"You and your younger brother."

"Yes, she didn't want to be a mother that late in life. She was happily single." Her aunt, while kindhearted, had been career minded and set in her ways. But her aunt had given them stability if not an abundance of motherly affection. "But she did her best by us."

"You brought up your brother."

"He means the world to me." She swallowed hard, then froze as a horrible thought hit her. "I hope you don't think I would ever have made a move on you to keep my job."

"No, God no. I know you better than that. You have always been a trustworthy person in the way you've handled business, the volunteers and the animals. I trust you, implicitly."

His praise and trust should make her feel good, but given the secret between them, she could barely hold back a wince of guilt.

"What happened between us that night was impulsive."

And impulsive was not her style. She didn't know how to roll with impetuous feelings. Ever since she'd become responsible for her younger brother, she had laid out a life plan. Put structure over desire because she had to. She didn't want to end up like her mother.

"But that night did happen, so why won't you speak to me?" He linked their fingers and rubbed the back of her hand against his stubbly jawline, holding her gaze as if he knew full well what that rasp against her skin did to her senses.

As if he knew full well how deeply attracted she was to him even as she sought to keep the boundaries high.

"I am speaking to you now."

"That's not what I meant and you know it." He kissed her fingers one at a time, and then lowered their clasped hands to rest on his knee. "But we can let that go for the moment. You were telling me about your mother."

"I told you already."

"You said she was first runner up for Miss Nevada. Why was that important?"

A loaded question.

Her mother had had full lips, long curly brown hair and the perfect hourglass figure. Conventionally beautiful. A fact her mom impressed upon Portia, who lacked those qualities. Her mother reminded her frequently that she was plain, average, in need of "sprucing up" with flashier clothes and makeup. Whereas her younger brother had a more classic cute kid look that her mom had insisted would make him a child television star.

Portia settled on a benign response. "She even made

it into the national pageant when Miss Nevada got pregnant and married during her reign. Mom didn't crack the top tier at nationals though."

"You're still not answering my question."

A lump grew in her throat. "Some parents play favorites. My brother was her favorite."

"That's not cool. Parents should love all their kids the same."

"Maybe I misspoke a bit. She loved me. She just... liked him better."

"Why?"

She plucked at the pillow in her lap. "He was everything she wanted in a child."

"How so?"

"Charismatic. Attractive." Her brother's eyes were deep brown, his skin always easily tanned. He could have been a child model. Compared to him, Portia had been disappointing.

"You're mesmerizing and gorgeous, and most importantly, brilliant."

"You don't need to stroke my ego. I told you. I'm comfortable in my skin. I don't need a centerfold body." This conversation had to end. Now. She didn't like this level of flattery. It set her on edge.

"You're beautiful."

"Stop—"

"I mean it. I've been clear about that." He looked at her with intense curiosity, lifting a rose from the vase on the table. Easton handed it to her, a romantic peace offering of sorts.

"Well, I did look like a drowned rat that night—" She stopped short.

"So we're finally going to talk about that night."

He leaped on her words, like he'd been waiting for any chance to discuss the night burned into her mind.

"I was there. I remember it well. Very well." For a moment, she imagined the feeling of his lips on hers, his hand twining in her hair and wrapping around her ponytail.

"As do I."

Five

After weeks of strained silence, Portia finally looked ready to discuss the night of the storm with him. Perhaps there would be an explanation for why she'd shut him out so completely since that night, and why she squirmed away from his compliments. Because damned if he was any closer to understanding this woman.

A knock at the door stayed her lips, causing them to shut tightly into a thin line. Easton was content to ignore the door, but she tipped her head in the direction of the continued tapping.

"Room service," Portia reminded him, starting to rise.

He'd already forgotten he'd ordered them dinner—a bread basket, herb-crusted red snapper, jasmine rice and side salads.

He grabbed her hand, gently tugging it. "Please, sit. I'll get it." He gestured for her to return to the tan couch or go to the small dining table. "Let me do something for you for a change. You're always running around keeping my life in order."

"Thank you. I appreciate it."

Good. He hoped so, because he was doing his best to salvage something from this disaster of a date.

Easton opened the door, met by a nervous-looking woman with bright red hair. She wheeled the overburdened cart into the center of the room and cast a glance at the rain-slicked window. Another crack of thunder sounded above them, sending vibrations through the building's foundation. The food attendant winced. The lights flickered and she shot them a faltering smile. "I thought it would be an adventure to move here." She quickly unloaded the food onto the table, and a blend of spices steamed into the air. "I'm ready to go back to shoveling snow. Um, sorry to babble."

"Please, don't apologize. We understand." Portia lifted lid after lid on the tray, inhaling. He heard her stomach growl in response, a blush rising to color her cheeks.

Even in the smallest moments, Easton found her drop-dead sexy.

The attendant nodded to Easton, and set three candles on the table. "Just in case we lose power." She took her tip and raced out of the room as if in search of the nearest transport north.

Easton pulled away the last of the covers, pleased with the results, especially considering how busy the hotel must be with the influx of guests due to the storm. "Come on, let's eat. You sound hungry after all."

"I'm going to pretend you didn't just insult my femininity." She fixed him with a dark look, but he saw the amusement in her eyes.

"Portia, your femininity has never been in question. I thought I made that abundantly clear two months ago. Unless you've forgotten about that night."

Her throat moved with a long swallow. "Of course I remember."

Good. Very good. "The rain sure sounds like that night."

He pulled out the rattan dining chair for her.

Another whack of thunder overhead. The lights strained brightly for a moment. A strange buzz erupted and the lights winked out. Easton grabbed the candles and matches, lighting the wicks. They hissed to life.

He was suddenly thankful for the lack of light. The flickering candle flame provided intimacy. Maybe the romantic date could be salvaged? Albeit in an unconventional way. But he never liked status quo anyway.

Portia bit into her roll, chewing thoughtfully. She swallowed before responding, eyes wandering past him to the window where raindrops beat onto the storm glass. "This tropical storm's nowhere near as bad as that one."

"I know. I guess it just sounds louder since we're not in a storm shelter," Easton agreed, stabbing a piece of snapper with his fork.

"It was secluded," Portia agreed, her eyes fixed on the flame. She looked up through her lashes. "And crowded."

And that wasn't his point, but at least she was talking.

The night with Portia had been all heat and fire. One that demanded attention and kindling. A draw he hadn't felt since his teenage years when he'd fallen hard for a girl in a village his family had hung around in for a whole four months—a time that had felt like forever to him as a teen. But as always, the next move was always in the works. He'd learned a lot about starting relationships, but not too much about how to maintain them. "It's a wonder we found a place to be alone and no one noticed we were gone.

"In case you're worried about gossip, I told the others you were nervous about the tropical storm since you're from Nevada, and I was reassuring you."

"Thank you."

"I would have told you as much if you would have spoken about that night before now."

"Well, you told me now. And I'm glad you stemmed any embarrassment."

"My brother was so caught up in his newfound love for Maureen I doubt he even heard me."

"They are a beautiful, happy couple. I didn't think there was a chance your brother would find someone after his wife died. He grieved so hard for Terri." A trace of sadness edged her voice. Portia had liked Terri, and he knew she was sad for little Rose to be growing up without her mother. The loss had devastated Xander and everyone at the refuge.

"Their marriage surprised me as well, and Maureen is so different from Terri, too." In fact, Easton had been more than surprised at his brother's interest in Maureen, Easton's quirky, outgoing second-in-command. Yet somehow, Xander and Maureen managed to make it work. "But there's no doubting how he feels about her."

"That's true." Portia pulled a weak smile. A roll of thunder sounded, lightning coursing through the room, dressing her slender face in shadows. Darkness lingered in her eyes.

He moved the candle to the center of the table. "You don't look like you agree."

"I do, then and now. I was just thinking how their romance made me feel." She shrugged. "I don't know, kind of sad that night, seeing them together."

"How so?" Tilting his head to the side, he leaned on his elbows, drawing ever-so-slightly closer to her.

"My life is such a mess I didn't think I would ever feel that way about someone." Portia sighed, that weak smile intact.

Easton raised a brow, confused. "You're the least messy person I've ever met."

She chased a piece of lettuce with her fork, a frown forming on her mouth. "My parents had an awful marriage. My brother, who I all but brought up, was barely keeping his head above water in school after a diagnosis of dyslexia. My plans for my life are on hold until he finishes college, and I can help him get his loans paid down. Then I'll go back to school."

"And what about now?"

She looked at him, a quiet resignation set in her brow. Everything about her stance looked defeated. "I'm not where I expected to be at this point in my life."

"Where would you like to be?" His voice dropped an octave, becoming gentler. Serious. He wanted her to know he was interested in what she wanted. Truly captivated by her.

"In college." She held up a hand. "But let's stop with that line of discussion. I don't want to talk about it. At all."

"Portia—"

"Seriously." She took a deep breath, shutting her eyes. "No. I don't want to discuss that. Let's talk about something else."

One strike and she'd already declared him out. But he didn't give up easily or play by the rules.

With nothing left to lose, he decided to gamble. Ask the question he'd most wanted the answer to. "Okay, how about you tell me why you didn't speak to me the day after the storm?"

"We were busy cleaning up the place." Her standard response was too calculated to be real.

"You really expect me to keep accepting that answer?" he asked with a laugh, trying to inject levity into this dark moment.

"It was worth a try." She smiled so wide her nose crinkled, then her grin faded.

"Nice. But I would really like an answer."

She tore at another piece of her bread. He watched her try to collect herself. "Okay, you're right that cleaning up after the storm just offered an excuse to keep my distance. The feelings were so intense that I worried if we repeated that night, I wouldn't be able to keep working with you." She set down her plate. "Now more than ever, I'm still not sure. And that's why we need to keep our distance."

In a flash, she'd scooped up a candle and her pink purse. The chair rocked slightly from her departure, and her footfalls were lost in the sustained rumble of thunder. Portia's hand covered the flame, bracing it from the air's assault.

Easton barely stood before she strode past the Jacuzzi and into the solitary bathroom. The door closed behind her slender back, coming into place with a definitive click.

The sound of a lock.

Damn.

He heard water rushing through pipes, and he imagined her—a siren amid the water's steam and bubbles.

She clearly needed space, but that image tortured him. Especially after the intensity of their roadside kiss and the honest answers she'd given him.

Deep breath.
Another.
One more. She ran the bathwater, trying to calm herself with the sound, but her heart pounded and she found herself blinking back tears.

With shaking hands, she pulled her cell phone from her purse. Her tired eyes squinted at the intense light of the screen as she found her brother Marshall's contact information.

One ring. Two. He should be picking up soon, up late studying for a test he'd told her about. Portia knew he was at school. He'd opted to take a summer class at University of West Florida in Pensacola in order to finish in five years rather than sliding over into a sixth.

The ringing stopped and the light sound of music filtered through the connection.

"Hey, sis." Marshall's voice was hoarse and distracted.

She imagined his lanky frame hunched over his desk, his dirty blond hair buzzed shorter these days so he could sleep later in the morning after staying up late studying.

"Do you have friends over? If you need to go, that's okay."

"I'm studying. You know how I like white noise in the background."

"I do remember." Her brother had had a tough time in school and she'd worked hard to help him stay on track. His grades hadn't been good enough for a scholarship and it was taking him an extra year to graduate. But as long as he finished, she would be happy.

"What can I do for you, sis?"

An excellent question. She had no idea what anyone could do for her. She hadn't even really had a reason to call Marshall. "I'm just calling to let you know I'm okay since the weather is so bad here."

"Um, the weather's bad there? I really have been locked down studying. I didn't even know there was a problem. Should I be on the lookout for a tropical storm or hurricane to swing my way?"

"I don't think so. It's just heavy rain. And maybe I needed to hear my little brother's voice." She poured bubbles into the tub, watched them grow, blanketing the top level of water.

"You're the best. Really. I appreciate it."

"Marshmallow—um, you don't mind if I still call you that, do you?"

His rich laughter made her smile. She was so damn proud of him.

"No problem, sis. Just don't post it online or anything."

"I wouldn't dare." She tested the water in the tub, appreciating the warmth.

"Thanks. And hey, be careful, okay?" A note of concern darkened his voice. "You work too hard and deserve a rest. I've been thinking I should take next year off and get a job, sock away some money and give you a break. You could go on a cruise or something."

Panic iced her. She loved her brother as much as if he were her own child—she'd practically raised him, after all. Held his hand as he learned to walk, wiped his tears when he scraped his knees, helped him with his spelling words. She feared if he stopped with school he would never go back. She'd seen it happen with other students, and she especially worried for him given how hard his learning disability made things for him. "Don't even entertain the notion. You are so close to finishing. Once you have your computer science degree, you're going to be so much more hirable. Just hang in there."

"We can talk at the end of the summer."

"You're going to break my heart if you don't finish. Please, see this through."

"What about you make me a promise as well to take care of yourself?"

"I will." She would have to tell Marshall about the baby soon, but not until he'd enrolled for the fall. She didn't want to distract him from his studies any sooner than necessary.

And of course, she still had to tell Easton, too. As soon as she had her doctor's appointment. One more week.

"Do you promise?" he pressed.

"Yes, I promise. I will relax. I went out to dinner tonight with, um, friends, and in fact, I have a bubble bath calling my name. So I should sign off. Love you."

"Love you, too."

She disconnected the call, putting the phone back in her purse, attention fully on the bath. She shimmied out of her clothes without the least thought of neatly folding them. For once, she had too much on her mind to care. The chill on her skin urged her to get beneath the blanket of warm water.

As she slid into the filling bath, her hands instinctively went to her stomach. She and Marshmallow would have a bigger family soon, a caring, close family. Another redeeming thought? This baby would offer her another chance to be a mom, this time an older and wiser one.

And what kind of father would Easton be? Involved? Distant? A playmate or educator?

She knew how he worked with a sense of fun and creativity, and she knew how he felt against her. Intensely focused on her needs and unwavering in his attention.

All of her thoughts led back to that night. The sustained thunder reminded her of the thunder from that other storm. How soothing Easton had been, how caring.

Portia inhaled deeply, listening to the sounds of the storm, watching the flame crackle to itself until her eyes grew heavy and she slipped into sleep...

Flashes of awareness entered her vision. As a non-Florida native, the power of the tropical storm terrified her. Easton's good-natured teasing shifted into pure comfort. In the storm shelter, he slid his arm around her.

That's when she felt yet again the undeniable heat between them at a time when she was too damn vulnerable. Marshall was close to failing out of college and losing hope that he could finish. She couldn't let her hard work and sacrifice be for nothing. She was scared for her brother's future. She was scared for her own future, listening to the storm rage.

Her defenses were down, and her heart was oh so vulnerable. She simply couldn't find the resolve to resist her attraction to Easton any longer. A passion she hadn't come close to feeling in her past two relationships with men, both more conventional types like her.

The attraction to Easton had burned into her with those blue-fire eyes, and before long, she wandered into the bathroom with him, first with a pointed look, then him following down the short hall to the tiny room with a simple shower stall.

They snuck in there, peeling themselves away from the others in the storm shelter.

"*Portia,*" *he said her name simply, the syllables so sexy coming from his mouth.*

"*No words. Just...*" *She couldn't find a way to express to him what she felt without giving away too much. She'd been attracted to his good looks from the start, but the physical was superficial. She'd been able to hold out, especially fearful of being seen as a gold digger like her mother.*

But over time, she'd been drawn all the more by his intelligence as well as his compassion around animals. Now here they were, acting on that attraction. She didn't want to think beyond that. She reached for him.

Or he reached for her. She wasn't sure who moved first. She only knew the attraction, the passion—the craving—was entirely mutual. Their first kiss felt like one of ultimate familiarity. Like coming home. Like one of a lover who'd known her for an eternity.

She wanted more. She wanted it all, regardless of where they were or how they'd ended up here or what tomorrow could hold because she couldn't think that far into the future. She whispered her need to him and he answered in kind as he lifted her onto the sink. She felt the ripples of his honed muscles as he managed the maneuver in an effortless sweep. He was such a fascinating mix of brains and brawn, privilege and earthiness.

"*You're so beautiful, so enchanting, so sexy. You've turned me inside out countless times with those take-no-bull eyes and the confident toss of your head. I've been burning to touch your hair, to take it down and feel it,*" *he whispered onto her skin with kisses, pressing his mouth into her flesh as his hands skimmed over her French twist. His fingers plucked at the pins and they clinked against the sink behind her one at a time as fast as her racing heart.*

Her mind blurred with passion. Their hands a frenzy as they pulled up shirts. Opened pants. Touched. Explored.

Found.

The room was dimly lit and small, his body close to hers with minimal room to step back. Yet driven by need she wriggled and he positioned. And he thrust inside her.

Her head fell back, a husky moan rolling up her throat. He captured it with his mouth, then skimmed a kiss along her ear, whispering gently shhh, shhh, shhh. Reminding her of the people a short hall away.

She dug her fingernails into Easton's shoulders, rolling her hips in sync with him, meeting him move for move. Their lovemaking ignited her every nerve, leaving her feeling, for the first time in a long time, connected.

For years, Portia had carefully constructed walls, pushed people outside to remain focused on providing a good life for her brother. She still wanted that. But she also wanted more. She wanted this. She wanted Easton.

Every kiss and every thrust reminded her of how lonely she'd been for years. For her whole life even. Each move and touch imprinted on her body and mind how exciting this was. How exciting they were together.

"Portia."

Her name sounded like a promise on his tongue, caressing her ear. Calming her senses but bringing her body to life. The beating of her heart sped up, becoming more ferocious and urgent.

And her name again. "Portia?"

No longer a promise, but a question...

* * *

Bolting upright awake, she grabbed the side of the tub and sloshed water over the sides, realizing she'd been asleep. Easton was, in fact, calling her name—but just from the other side of the door. Portia looked across the bathroom, a different and more spacious one than in her dream.

The bathwater had cooled, chilling her overheated flesh. She glanced at the door, then down to the haphazard pile of her clothes on the tile floor. Water pooled along the Saltillo squares. A lot of water. She must have splashed and thrashed during her nap in the tub leaving her clothes totally soggy...

And impossible to wear.

Easton rapped his knuckles on the door. Portia had scurried away an hour ago. In the last ten minutes, his desire to give her space ebbed, replaced by worry. He'd imagined her sick, or passed out on the floor.

"Portia? Are you okay? I'm getting worried." He called again, fingering the plush white hotel robe he held ready for her, "Portia, answer please or I'm going to need to open the door."

"I'm okay."

Finally. Thank God. The sound of her husky voice soothed him slightly.

"I'm sorry for disturbing your bath." He pressed his forehead to the door in relief, the cool wood soothing his overheated brow. "I apologize for upsetting you into bolting away earlier. I don't know what I said, but you have to know I would never deliberately hurt you."

"I'm really okay."

Still, he couldn't step away. "Are you going to spend the night in there?"

"Of course not."

"Do you plan to come out anytime soon?" He angled back and stared at the door, as if that act alone would cause it to swing open.

"I was thinking I would come back in there right after you go to sleep."

"Well, that's a problem because there's only one bathroom in here and I'm going to need to step in there before bed. Or rather before I go to sleep on the sofa."

"Oh, of course. I'm sorry about that. I'll be right out."

More rustling water sounds echoed, followed by drips of water. The lock popped open, and she stood in front of him. Damp tangled hazelnut hair, the small white towel wrapped around her, accentuating her curves.

Air pulled away from him. Damn, she was sexy. She turned him inside out in a way he remembered well from their night together but he had wondered if his memory was faulty.

He had tried his best to get answers from her. To be a gentleman. To get closer to her on a more cerebral level.

But that hadn't gotten him jack squat. He didn't understand her any more now than he ever had. But he recognized the heat between them. And damned if he didn't see that same simmering warmth reflected in her eyes.

On to Plan B.

Hungry for her touch, he reached for Portia.

Six

His lips found hers, catching her by surprise until she almost stumbled back into the bathroom.

All the tension she'd been storing in her body seemed to flood out of her as she unfolded into the moment. In the taste of his lips, the curve of his tongue. Her nerves melted, all tension over thoughts of meeting him in only a towel leaving her.

For this evening, here in this hotel honeymoon suite she could be a little foolish. Give in to the chemistry between them. Hell, she wanted him. Like with the kiss in the car, she didn't have much time to be with him, to get to know him, to explore every inch of him. Because her plan to put boundaries between them wasn't going to work. It wasn't boss and secretary time, not anymore.

She would have to find her way to a new peace with him. She would have to find a way to have him and her independence, too. And while this might seem reckless, playing it safe hadn't worked. And once the news of her pregnancy came out, her window of time to explore avenues for connecting with him would narrow. Considerably.

He sighed heavy against her, taking a step back deeper into the living area. Closer to the sprawling bed. A rush of cold air pressed against her chest and neck, a palpable absence. "I'm sorry. I didn't mean to grab for you like a caveman. I saw you in the towel and, well, damn, I couldn't think straight." He nodded past her, toward the bathroom. "I realize now your clothes are damp and hanging out to dry. You didn't have a choice but to wear the towel."

She leaned into him, the rain-fresh scent of him tempting her all the more. "If I'd wanted you to stop kissing me, I would have said so."

His eyebrows shot upward. "Really?"

"Really. I'm a mature woman. I know what I want and I am capable of speaking my mind." At least, for right now, she knew she needed his touch. All of him. Reality could wait until the sunrise.

"And what would that be? I need to hear you say what you want before I make another move."

"I want you." She stepped back, closer to the bed, unable to miss the way his eyes lingered on her long hair falling in damp and loose strands. "Right now, I want you to keep kissing me and more. I want us to explore the attraction we found that night of the tropical storm. To take it further and take our time. I wasn't planning this, but let's see where it goes."

"Well, I'm very glad to hear that since I want you, too. So damn much." He reached for her and she took another step back. He tipped his head, intensity stamped all over his face. "Are you going to drop the towel?"

"Are you going to undress for me?" Her gaze roamed over his muscled body, wanting to see and feel more of him.

"My pleasure." He began unbuttoning his shirt.

"I believe it will be mine. We didn't get to see each other before." So much of the sensations of the night had been lost to frenzy. She wanted to know every inch of him.

"No, we didn't." He tossed aside his cotton button-down, revealing the sun-bronzed chest she'd admired more than once while he'd been swimming. "I'm not arguing with you by any means, but what brought about this change of heart?"

"Do you need to know why? Can it be enough to know I want to be close to you tonight? Because I do, so very much." She gripped the towel in her fist, holding it closed as the water nearly steam dried off her warming body. "This day may not have been what we planned, but I have enjoyed being with you. I'm not ready for it to end."

"Portia…" He gritted his teeth, obviously wanting to say more.

"That's all I can give," she answered softly, honest in this much at least.

He gave in with a growl of frustration and desire. "Okay, beautiful lady, that's good enough for me tonight."

He toed off his shoes and tugged off his socks.

His hand fell to his belt buckle and then to the zipper of his khakis. He kicked his pants aside and there was nothing left between them except her towel and his boxers. His erection strained the waistband, attesting to just how much he wanted her.

The towel slid from her grip and his eyes went wide with appreciation. A step later from her—from him—and they stood chest to chest, mouths meeting.

His hand wandered to her damp hair, the movement bringing them closer. Easton kissed her, tongue exploring, urgency mounting. Her hands outlined circling swirls on his skin, enjoying the way he seemed to respond to her touch. His kiss becoming more urgent with every sweep of her fingertips.

He walked her backward toward the bed until her legs met the mattress. A gentle nudge sent her onto her back—into the downy blue duvet, pillows scattering.

She pulled back from him, eyes adjusting to the dim light, appreciating his body and the hungry look in his eyes. Portia stared up at him through her lashes, worried he might notice the changes in her body, in particular the swell of her breasts. Or would he just write off the differences to mistaken memory over time? Or perhaps to the fact that they hadn't even had the opportunity to look closely enough that night? She certainly hadn't been able to gaze her fill of him.

He leaned her back on the bed, the coolness of the cotton bedspread pressing against her skin—a stark contrast to the heat of his body. Wandering lips found her collarbone, and her hands tugged at his boxers, pulling them off. He angled on top of her.

His hand tucked between her legs, his fingers finding the damp core of her, stroking and coaxing and dipping inside. His touch slickened; he rubbed over the bud of her arousal.

Tonight was already so different from the evening of the other storm, the night they'd quickly and impulsively made love. Every kiss tonight was more deliberate, more passionate. She bit his lower lip, and he growled in response, pressing into her. She hooked her right leg around his, needing him to get closer. Her heart bolted at a maddening pace, her excitement intensifying as his hands brushed back her hair so he could kiss her neck. Her lips.

Palming his chest, she traced him with her other hand, trailing down, down, farther still until she cupped his straining need, wrapping her fingers around the length of him. A groan of pleasure hissed from between his teeth just before he pressed his lips to hers again.

He stole her breath, and she stole his right back. Their tongues met, thrusted and stroked just as their hands touched and caressed each other. Each touch brought her closer to completion and his quickening breaths between kisses told her he was equally near the edge.

She wondered when he would call a stop to this and reach for the honeymoon suite gift basket by their bed—a basket with condoms in every color imaginable. But he showed no signs of stopping.

With knowing hands, he kept touching her, pushing her toward the edge, interspersing deep kisses with roving hands. Driving her wild. He took her closer to release, then eased up, only to tease her closer again. And she reveled in tempting him in equal measure, stroking and stroking, grazing her thumb over the head of his erection. The first droplets of his impending release slicked over the tip, giving her the power to move faster, his breath speeding in time. Thank goodness. Because she didn't know how much longer she could hold back...

Bliss.

Pulse after pulse of pleasure ripped through her, and she only barely kept her wits around her enough to bring him to his release, as well. His deep groan caressed her ears bringing a fresh wave of aftershocks shimmering along her passion-sensitive nerves.

As the last tremble faded, she sagged back, gasping from the power of her orgasm. She couldn't even find the will to open her eyes just yet. She could only feel.

A rustle sounded beside her. Easton. The covers shifted as he untangled them from their feet, and then a sheet settled along her. The ceiling fan overhead sent gusts of air down to dry the perspiration along her forehead.

Easton settled beside her, and she glanced at him, rolling to her side. His arm was flung over his eyes, his chest rising and falling rapidly, each breath a hint slower but still not back to normal. She reveled in the knowledge she'd brought him the same pleasure he'd given her.

Her eyes drifted to the honeymoon suite gift basket by their bed, looking at the assortment of neon condoms. Was that glitter on them, as well? A hint of apprehension whispered through her. She wasn't ready to tell him that they didn't need condoms.

Now she just had to figure out how to deal with using glitter-covered birth control.

The moment felt like an eternity as she stared at the basket, contemplating how to proceed. Heart hammering, Portia felt her hands start to tingle, a sure sign of her anxiety.

Easton's deep blue eyes searched her face. "Come here."

He opened his arms to her.

She hesitated.

He lifted her hand and tugged her gently until she toppled to rest against his chest. His arms folded around her and anchored her there. "Sleep."

Surprise drifted through her passion-fogged mind as she realized somehow he'd understood her hesitation even though she hadn't voiced it. "You're serious? You don't want to finish this?"

"I do. But I can tell you're not ready and I'm smart enough not to make the same mistake twice. You're too important to me."

His words touched her as intensely as any stroke against her skin.

"If you're sure?"

"I am. Very." He rubbed her bare shoulder gently. "Now rest. We'll talk more tomorrow."

He draped himself around her, encircling her in his muscled arms. Protective and gentle.

She settled into him, noting the rhythmic rise and fall of his chest. The darkness in the room covering them both, shielding them from the reality of the morning. But for right now, Portia could pretend everything was fine and normal. That having someone take care of her was exactly what she needed.

And it was damn hard to deny that this didn't feel natural.

Morning sun streaking through the shutters, Easton listened to the patter of the shower and thought of the night before when Portia had been in that same bathroom, soaking in the tub.

They'd never made it to the spa in the corner of their bedroom, the ledge decorated with candles and champagne. But then this was a honeymoon suite, and they were not honeymooners.

He scratched his chest and kicked aside the covers. While all his plans for the evening hadn't come to fruition, he had no regrets. He'd made significant progress in his hopes of winning his way back into her bed.

Instinct told him the best move was to give her space. To pursue her carefully so as not to scare her off again. He wasn't risking this second chance to be with her. He knew too well how fast life could change, how quickly people he thought he could count on were gone. He also knew his own shortcomings in maintaining relationships for the long haul.

He swung his legs off the mattress, feet meeting the cool floor. He tugged on his boxers and reached into his pants pocket for his cell. After that storm, he should check in with Maureen and make sure the refuge hadn't suffered substantial damage. While he loved spending the night with Portia, he knew the staff and animals at the preserve counted on him.

Walking out to the balcony, he cued up Maureen's number. The Gulf Coast waters glistened in the aftermath of the storm. A few branches littered the beach and chairs were overturned, but he didn't see any major upheaval. Morning walkers and shell collectors were already on the sand, a few kids dodging waves in bathing suits and tiny life vests. Vacationers were getting back to normal. Hopefully he would get the same report from home. Maureen answered on the third ring, her voice bright and alert.

"How'd we fare with that storm last night?" Easton asked in lieu of a normal introduction.

"And good morning to you, too," Maureen teased. "We've been worse this year. Some debris, naturally. I'm mobilizing a team of volunteers for yard cleanup."

Easton sank into one of the wooden Adirondack

chairs, looking out onto the sun-speckled water. "How about the animals?"

"Spooked a few of them. But no substantial damage to any of the facilities and no major injuries to speak of," Maureen said, a parrot cawing in the background. "We were lucky."

"That's great to hear. I worried about them and you guys." He inhaled deeply, the scent of ocean overpowering his senses.

"So are you transporting any animals on your way back up?" Maureen asked.

"No. This isn't exactly a business trip."

He could practically see Maureen's eyebrows raising as she responded. "Yeah. I guessed that. Easton?"

"What?"

"Be careful with Portia. I think she is going through something. She's just been off lately. At first, I thought she was worried about how Marshall was doing in college, but now I'm not so certain that's the only concern in her life."

Protectiveness crept through him, making him want to scoop her up and handle any worries that burdened her. He *would* figure them out, damn it. "Thanks for the heads-up."

"We all care about her. She's more than an employee."

"I know. I'll talk to her today on our way back. See you soon." He ended the call, looking through the sliding glass door, Maureen's words echoing in his mind. He had noticed the same thing about Portia more than once lately.

But he'd failed to take action in helping her. He'd been so focused on his own pursuit, his own needs. Guilt stung.

Easton went back inside and practically ran into Portia. Her hair was damp and loose from her shower, but rather than a towel, this time she was dressed in her clothes from yesterday. They were wrinkled, but dry. He didn't want to rush her, especially not after he'd just made a point of deciding to give her space.

No caveman tactics today. He would take things slow.

But she looked gray, like the color had been leeched from her. Her eyes briefly met his, but she turned away to perch on the edge of the sofa as if ready to take flight.

With a doctor's eye—even if for animals rather than people—he studied her more closely. Looked into her eyes. Counted her respiration as well as her pulse throbbing along her neck. And still he was no closer to figuring out what had upset her.

He could heal any animal, identify birds by their songs, but determining what made Portia tick was proving to be much more challenging.

Noting the exhaustion on her pale face, he said the first thing that came to mind, "You've been putting off going to school because of your brother's loans. What if I told you that you don't have to wait?"

"What do you mean?"

"Plenty of bosses help pay for their employees' college education. So why not start classes now?"

"I'm not the kind of woman who will take money from a man she's seeing, much less sleeping with, and it's insulting that you think I would." Fire burned in her eyes.

And her response struck a nerve for him.

"I'm insulted you think I would offer for any reason other than wanting to help. I should have thought to learn more about you sooner, and I would have known the need." He clasped her shoulders in a gentle grip and hoped she would read the genuine concern in his eyes. "Clearly stress is wearing you down and if you're burned out then that's bad for me on many levels. As a boss and as a person who cares about you. So let me help how I can."

"No." She shook her head, lips tight.

"That's it? No?" His hands dropping to his sides, he stepped away, and paced for a moment until he caught his betraying restlessness and leaned against the doorframe, trying his best not to appear frustrated. Easton wanted the best for Portia. No strings attached. He cared about her.

"Yes." She tugged her hair scrunchie off her wrist.

"Good."

"No, I meant, no you can't help." She piled her hair into a high ponytail on the top of her head, pulling it tight. "And yes, my answer is still no."

"Would you care to expand on that?"

She sagged into a chair. "Another time?"

Every road led back to this with her—to him being shut out like last time. As if she was leaving before she even had a chance to inevitably head out the door. "Sure, but on one condition."

"What's that?"

"You won't close yourself off again and block me out completely," he said, a gentle demand. He searched her face to gauge her reaction.

Portia's eyes fluttered shut. For a moment, she didn't speak. A sigh escaped her, and she opened her eyes to stare at him. "That's not a promise to sleep together. Last night—"

"Was another impulsive moment." He completed the sentence for her, finding he actually agreed with her. Stepping closer, he continued, "I get that. Completely. That's why we didn't finish."

"Truly?" She played with her necklace, sliding the charm back and forth on the silver chain.

"Yes, Portia. Truly. I want you to have sex with me totally aware of what we're doing. Not swept away. Well, swept away, but for all the right reasons. And trust me, I do believe that will happen and in the not too distant future."

"You're mighty confident." The first hint of a smile shone in her eyes, tipping her beautiful lips and chasing away some of the strains of exhaustion.

"About what we're feeling? Yes, I am." He lifted her hand and pressed a kiss to the inside of her wrist, lingering, holding her eyes for an instant before linking their fingers and stepping back. "Now let's get dressed and hit the road. We're both going to be late for work."

The ride back to the refuge had been mostly silent. Portia organized her notes, working hard as they drove.

As she color-coded her tasks, she felt more settled. This process with her notes and highlighters provided order and grounding. Each precise stroke of the pen and marker helped erect her protective walls.

Easton hadn't pressed her during the ride, letting her work in silence while he guided the low-slung Corvette around the storm-tossed debris on the roads. He hadn't even argued when she'd bypassed breakfast and asked only for warm tea with peppermint. Although she had pretended to nibble on a cookie.

She looked up from her planner, the afternoon sun warming her skin. They were on the road to the refuge. Somehow, two hours had come and gone.

He pulled the Corvette into the driveway, parking beneath a tall royal palm tree. They unbuckled, each exiting the vehicle. When her foot touched the solid ground, Portia's nerve and resolve grew.

She wasn't normally a person of impulse but after last night, she wondered if perhaps she should tell him about the baby now after all.

"Um, Easton," she began, hesitantly, words catching in the air as Maureen bounded onto the scene.

Portia couldn't ignore the huge sense of relief over being let off the hook a little while longer. Yes, she selfishly wanted more time with Easton to explore this attraction before risking a possible confrontation when he found out about their child.

"Hey pretty lady, you're back. I have a surprise planned for us." Maureen beamed at her, wrapping Portia in a hug. "I'm stealing your assistant for the remainder of the day. And your brother wants to talk to you." Maureen laughed, pulling Portia to the door of the mansion.

"You two have fun. Portia, we'll talk more later." He waved. Heading toward the clinic.

Maureen tugged Portia into the mansion toward the spacious women's locker room. She put her hands over Portia's eyes as she led her inside.

Relaxing harp music sounded, and when Maureen removed her hands, Portia took in the transformation. The steel and oak-benched locker room had been transformed into a day spa, not just with softer lighting, candles and sparkling water, but complete with pink-draped massage tables, a table of dainty foods, and makeup/hairstylist gear.

Maureen spread her arms wide. "Surprise. I knew you would try to go back to work after the time away, so I caught up with everything at the clinic. Now we can enjoy a girls' getaway, complete with dinner and pampering. Facials and shoulder massages and even a hair trim."

Portia froze, indecision and old insecurities taking

control. "I appreciate your generosity, but I'm not comfortable with a makeover."

"That's not what this is about at all. You're beautiful as you are. I meant what I said about pampering only. You work too hard."

Maureen pointed to the spread of food on the far table.

Portia pursed her lips, leery of trusting Maureen. She felt vulnerable. But the food smelled divine. The long wooden table had a mixture of breads, garlic-crusted chicken, crab legs, and angel-hair pasta with lemon butter. Portia's stomach growled in response.

Now that Portia's stomach had settled and since she hadn't eaten yet today, the meal tempted her as much as the prospect of a shoulder massage.

"You have beautiful hair. Why do you keep it pulled back? It looks almost painful."

"It isn't." She touched her ponytail self-consciously.

"I'm sorry." Maureen winced. "I shouldn't have said anything. That was rude of me. I just wondered…but it's none of my business."

"I actually have my mother's hair." Portia stepped up into the stylist chair, looking at her reflection in the mirror. She shrugged her shoulders.

"And that's not good?"

"We had our differences, many of them. In fact, we were different in every way except for our thick hair— if not the same color. I want to be my own person so I chose a different style than hers."

"Then be your own person. Take charge."

"I have." Mostly. Partly. She'd brought up Marshall. She'd provided for him, a contrast from her mother's version of caring, which involved making sure they had the right "look." Their mom's pampering of her son had been almost smothering as she paraded her little boy in front of agents in hopes of landing a child star role in a commercial or television show. Portia felt that lack of a normal childhood could have been at least as damaging as the criticism she'd received. And then after their mother's death when Portia and Marshall had gone to live with their aunt in Florida, the decidedly nonmaternal woman had used what bit of parenting instincts she had to parent the younger of the two, leaving teenage Portia to fend for herself as she navigated young adulthood.

"Okay." Maureen nodded, slicing a mix of cheeses from the assortment and sliding the samplings onto the bone china plate along with fruit and crackers. She brought it to Portia, a smile resting on her lips. "Good?"

"Looks delicious." Portia took the delicate dish, wary of Maureen's easy acquiescence. "Just okay? You aren't going to push me to participate in some magic makeover?"

"Remember! Today is *not* about makeovers. It's about relaxation and letting our inner self shine through." Maureen plucked up a grape and popped it into her mouth.

"But you want to offer advice."

"Of course. I'm opinionated." She snorted on a laugh. "Just ask my husband. Or anyone who knows me for more than five minutes then, like you."

"Alright, then. Let it fly. I'm a canvas." She popped a cheese cracker into her mouth before setting aside the china. "Paint me."

Maureen sat back in her chair, examining Portia. "I would suggest you let your hair down and quit thinking about your mother. Embrace who you are. Your hair doesn't have to be up or completely down either. I realize you like it back from your face. So perhaps try some clips, have fun with jewelry."

"That's it? Let my hair down and pack some Be-Dazzled pins?" She was surprised, half imagining that Maureen was going to suggest a severe haircut or worse—bleach it as her mom had not-too-subtly suggested more than once.

Well, damn. She did think about her mother's criticisms too often.

"It's a start, Portia. If you could choose any dress you wanted, no holds barred, what would you choose?" She gestured wide with her hands, as if all the clothes in the world were actually in front of them.

"I thought you were supposed to be helping me pick."

"I will, if you need me, but I don't think you need anyone's guidance on this."

Portia glanced back over her shoulder, curious and a little suspicious of some mystery motive. "What's really going on here? Did Easton put you up to this?"

Or worse yet, after their night spent away, was Maureen attempting to matchmake?

"I'm just empowering you to be who you want to be." Maureen removed Portia's ponytail, letting her heavy hair fall. Grabbing a brush, she worked through her tangled air-dried locks. "Oh Lord, did I really just say that? Empowering? I sound like some kind of self-help book—you're the last woman who needs help. I just want to pamper you since you go out of your way to take care of others. And in case you're worried, the professional hairstylist will be here soon."

"It's kind of you to arrange all of this, and I don't mean to sound like an ingrate." She looked at her short, neat nails and wondered what they would look like with a bolder color, not long French tips or fake nails, but just something...fun. "I shouldn't have said what I did about my mother. I don't want to be someone who blames everyone else for my hang-ups."

Maureen set down the brush and took a chair beside her. "You're the last person I would assume that about. You are levelheaded and confident."

Portia didn't feel that way. She felt like she'd clawed her way through life to find confidence and a future for herself and her brother. To find the independence she craved. She didn't want this roaring frustration inside her. She wanted to be happy about this baby, her child. Instead, she was just...scared.

What did she know about being a mother? She hadn't had good examples. Maybe this spa day, and the time with Easton, would help her get her head on straight before her whole world changed.

The doctor's appointment was less than a week away. A relief.

And the ticking clock counting down her time to finish exploring this whole empowerment exercise. Soon she would take on the whole Lourdes family full force—and one incredibly charming veterinarian—and tell them she was carrying the next little addition.

Seven

Three hours later, Easton stood in the doorway leading to the women's locker room and braced his hands on either side to keep his footing. He'd heard from his brother that the women were getting dinner, massages and makeovers. And he'd expected some glammed up, artificial look. He'd prepared himself to say the right things on his way to kissing the artifice away. Had anticipated the moment with a raw sensuality that burned deep inside him.

However, he hadn't expected Portia's angled features to make her look downright ethereal. And the difference rocked him. He'd always found her attractive—her kindness, her stunning smile, her deep, dark eyes.

But with her hair falling around her ears…

How she sat relaxed and causal…

She knocked the air from his lungs. Literally.

Her eyes widened as she noticed his stare, a faint blush

rising, swirling in her cheeks. The shadowed light catching on her slender face. Damn.

"You look stunning," Easton said, his voice hoarse as he worked to drag air into his lungs again. "And I don't just mean the hair or the makeup. There's a glow to you that's incredible."

Maureen tipped her head to the side. "A glow?"

Portia shot to her feet, dismissive of his compliment. "Thank you. All the credit goes to the makeup artist and hairstylist. I just sat still and let them work."

She walked to the drink station and fixed herself a glass of sparkling water and then dropped in a lime slice from a bowl.

Don the security guard and his wife, Jessie, floated into the room. Active fiftysomethings, they were a powerhouse volunteer couple. They donated a substantial amount of time and money to the refuge. Somehow, they'd also become surrogate grandparents to Rose, poking in and out of the house. Down-to-earth people no one would suspect actually had made billions through savvy investments in the dot-com world, getting out right before it crashed. They were a regular fixture around here, often staying late. It was never a surprise to see them wander in, and the Lourdes family could never pay them back for all they'd done for the refuge.

The dim light of the room made Jessie's spotted pullover appear like a molten mix of tan and black, making her seem like a jungle cat. Elbows hooked together, they strode over to Easton and Portia who had shrugged off her robe to reveal a formfitting mint dress. All of her curves accented, the mint color brought her pale skin to life. Teasing him, tempting him.

She brushed her fingers against his. A small gesture, sure. But he found himself itching for more. A lot more.

Jessie cooed, patting Don's stomach. "Did y'all know that we are celebrating thirty-three years of marriage next week?"

"That is amazing." Portia nodded, a smile on her lightly glossed lips.

Easton nodded absently as well, eyes fixed on her. Wanting her.

"Are you doing anything special?" Easton said after a moment, shifting his weight slightly so his body would caress Portia's. She leaned into him, like a palm tree swaying in a springtime breeze. Awareness simmered between them, a slow burn.

Don combed his fingers through his snow-gray hair. "When are you planning to ask her out on an official date?"

Portia choked on her sip of sparkling water.

Easton set his drink aside slowly and lifted an eyebrow. "When did you start up a matchmaking service?"

Don shrugged, proceeding in his typical straightforward manner. He'd never been one to mask his thoughts or feelings. "Sorry to have put the two of you on the spot there, but it's obvious to all of us around here that the two of you are an item. So I was just wondering when you're going to start dating. Or if you already are, let the rest of us in on it so we can double date."

"Double date?" Portia squeaked, putting aside her own drink now.

Jessie reached her hand out to gently squeeze Portia's arm. She gave a quick wink. "Sure. Do you think married couples don't date anymore? If that's your idea of marriage, no wonder you've stayed single for so long."

Easton watched as color drained from Portia's face. He decided to steer the conversation to a different topic— anything to make Portia feel more comfortable and not derail his plan to win her back into his bed. "I know married couples have romance. I've seen my brother married twice, happily both times."

Jessie lowered her voice, holding a glass of sparkling wine in a relaxed grasp. "Then you two are dating and keeping it quiet?"

She asked so casually, as if she were inquiring about the weather and not asking for a piece of private, intimate information.

Easton folded his arms over his chest, frustrated that his friends could be eroding the progress he'd made toward getting Portia back into his bed. "No offense, Don, but why is this any of your business?"

"Wow, you're in a bad mood. Must be the barometric pressure drop," Don teased, still not getting the message. Easton saw Portia's spine grow rigid, the glow of earlier replaced by seething discomfort.

Jessie gave an exaggerated wink. "Or a lack of romance in your life."

Portia waved a hand. "Hello, I'm here and a part of this conversation."

Jessie turned to Portia, blinking. In faux seriousness, she asked, "So is he properly romancing you?"

Easton held up a hand. "Stop. Yes, I'm interested, very interested, in Portia. And I want to win her over, but that's for her to say and you're not helping matters."

All eyes turned to Portia.

"What?" She held up her hands defensively. "Things are complicated."

Jessie nodded. "He's your boss."

"True." Portia winced. "Thanks for reminding me."

Easton had kept his frustration under control when it was all good-natured ribbing, but now, as he watched Portia grow increasingly uncomfortable, he started to steam. He wanted to protect her from any upset, even something as innocent as this sort of thing.

Jessie shot a warning look at Easton before leaning toward Portia. "Has he made you uncomfortable with his advances? Because that wouldn't be right."

Easton bristled. Established, wealthy volunteers or not, there were lines and they were skirting close to crossing them.

Portia touched his arm lightly. "Easton hasn't done anything wrong. I made the first move on him, okay? So there. Yes, we have feelings for each other. Yes, we're attracted to each other. And yes, it was probably silly of us to think our private lives could be private in such an intimate work environment, but we really would appreciate some space to figure this out. Thank you."

She adjusted her weight and fixed them both with a commanding stare before striding out of the room. Her chin up.

He had never seen her be so assertive before. She'd become a force—like the storms that had brought them together—firm, unflinching and unapologetic.

Dazzling.

And he was stunned as hell that he wanted more than just to have her back in his bed again.

Drained, Portia sagged against the door after the men left, watching the stylist pack her gear, listening to the sounds of zippers and bottles of products clinking together before more footsteps reverberated along with the closing of a door. With the portable salon packed in bags, the room echoed.

She hadn't been in the mood for such prying questions from anyone, even friends like Don and Jessie. And the questions seemed to carry more weight, hit her more deeply, because of her pregnancy.

Her still secret pregnancy, made all the more complicated by that look in Easton's eyes when he'd seen her. She could have sworn she saw more than just passion, and that excited her and scared her all at once because heaven help them, this could not be a regular dating relationship. They didn't have the luxury.

Pressing a hand to her forehead and closing her eyes, she couldn't remember the last time she'd felt so alone. Then the warm press of another person sidled beside her, sweeping an arm around her shoulder. Portia looked over, the smell of peonies and powder lingering.

Jessie. A woman happily married for decades. A grandmother. Content with where she was in her life.

A painful sight for Portia right now.

The older woman patted Portia's shoulder. "I'm sorry, dear, we didn't mean to upset you. My man, he can be pushy, but he didn't mean any harm. We thought it was so obvious."

Portia found it easy to forgive the woman for her overreaching. Jessie showed her tender heart daily in how she sang to wounded animals as they underwent treatment. Which made her think of Easton's tender care of animals that could seriously injure him in their wounded, frantic state. He was such an intriguing, unexpected sort of person.

She looked down at her fingers twisted together in her lap. "Our feelings are that apparent?"

Maureen's brogue answered as she called from behind a changing screen, "Yes, they are. Especially this past week." She passed Portia a tissue. "I've never seen you cry before."

Portia sagged onto an oaken locker room bench. "I do have emotions."

Sitting beside her, Jessie stroked a lock of hair over Portia's shoulder. "Of course you do. You just usually keep them to yourself. But those feelings are tougher to keep inside when hormones are out of control."

Jessie gave her a pointed look that all but had Portia squirming in her chair. Her secret pregnancy wouldn't be a secret much longer if people were already guessing. Luckily, Maureen seemed oblivious. Still, the time clock was ticking down. Portia had to tell Easton. "I'm doing better now, but thank you for caring.

"Of course, dear, we're all a big family here. And I'll make sure Don lightens up on the teasing." Jessie clucked her tongue like a protective mother hen.

"Thank you. That would be helpful." Especially until Portia figured things out for her future as a mother.

With a satisfied nod, Jessie stood up. She fluffed her hair with her fingers, and started to walk away. She paused for a moment, spinning on her kitten heels to face Portia. "You really are lovely, and glowing. Take care of yourself, dear. Maureen, would you mind taking me to see my favorite little Key deer baby that has a broken leg?"

Maureen pranced out from behind the screen, her curly red hair falling midchest, contrasting with her white shift dress. Her gold accessories catching the light, making her look like some Celtic princess from centuries past.

"Of course. I have about an hour before I'm supposed to meet Xander. I'll take you to the baby deer."

She linked her arm with Jessie's and tossed Portia a wave and a wink.

Glowy.

Such an intentional and loaded word.

Did they know? Or at the very least suspect?

Before panic could fully rise in her chest, Portia's cell phone rang, sending her thoughts skittering. Looking down at the screen, she read *Marshall*.

Scrambling to answer, she clicked the green button, shoving the phone to her ear.

"Hey, sis. I haven't heard from you in a while—"

"Since last night."

"I know," he teased gently. "I was being sarcastic. You sounded, um, off last night. I wanted to follow up. You're not the only one who worries."

The weight of responsibility felt heavier than ever on her shoulders. Every decision she made could have such far-reaching repercussions. "Work has been hectic. How are you?"

"I'm good. Classes are good, grades are solid and I have good news for you."

"I could use good news." She couldn't keep a wobble of concern out of her voice. She was so confused, and for a woman used to controlling every inch of her life, that was a difficult and alien way to feel.

"Are you sure you're okay?"

Oh, nothing. Just my life being torn apart.

She wanted to say something like that—wanted to share her life-altering news with her brother. Instead, she looked at her nails, choosing to remain the strong, balanced force she always thought Marshall needed. "Yes, of course. Tell me your news?"

"I got a gig as a residence hall counselor after summer session this fall, which means free dorm and a break on tuition. There's been a last-minute opening and they asked me."

"That's fantastic." A shred of positive news. There'd be less to siphon away from her pay. The debt for his college education was worth it though. She needed to see him settled before she could make any plans for her future, however much she wanted to... She stopped thoughts of Easton short. For now. And she focused on her brother's words instead.

"I'm trying my best not to be a burden to you. I appreciate all you've done for me."

"It's my joy. I'm proud of you." She'd never told him of her own dreams to go to college. She was so afraid if he didn't complete his education now he never would. She needed to know he was secure in his future.

But she also had a child to consider. Life was so very complicated.

And she wanted to be with Easton again so damn much.

The next day, when Easton had asked her to have dinner by the pool after work, she hadn't even bothered making an excuse to decline. Clearly, hiding their mutual interest from everyone and each other was futile. In a way, that observation caused a degree of relief for Portia. There would be no sneaking around now. Fewer secrets. This would be their first date since their night in the inn. The night they'd almost slept together.

A night she couldn't get out of her mind.

After his date request, she'd rushed to her cabana to shower and change. As she slipped into a simple backless green dress, she felt a buzz hum through her body.

Apprehension coursed through her spine, filling her with a strange mixture of curiosity and desire. She fluffed her hair, opting to let it stay down like the stylist had done the day before.

Maybe there was something to all that empowerment talk Maureen had given Portia. A new hairstyle for a new chapter in her life. The small change felt like she'd made a promise to herself to be brave for her own future and not just for her brother.

Regardless of the attraction between her and Easton, Portia needed to get to know him better. The father of her unborn child. No. Wait. That was wrong.

Their unborn child.

That shared child meant they would forever be in each other's lives, even if he was a reluctant parent. She couldn't see him turning his back on his child altogether. And if he did? Then he wasn't a man worthy of either of them.

She left her little home and walked the path over to the pool by the main house. Easton had said he planned to walk her over, but coming to him gave her more of a sense of power.

Now she was glad she had done so as she had a few minutes to take in the dinner arrangements unobserved. Easton had hired a Spanish guitarist and a pianist to play sultry songs. The beautiful riffs filled the night air, making her forget for a moment that she was at his house and not in some fancy restaurant.

Glancing around the pool deck, she certainly felt like

they had been transported somewhere magical. High romance. No expense spared. Globe lights were strung overhead like personal stars. The whole patio was decorated in hibiscus flowers and soft green ferns—a tropical getaway in the middle of daily life.

The house was silent and unlit. Xander, Maureen and baby Rose had left for an evening getaway.

Easton stepped through the double French doors with a bouquet of peonies in his hand and stopped short once he saw her, then he picked up his pace again.

"Portia," he called out, "I wanted to escort you over."

She met him at the stairs. "I know, but I was ready early, and I do know where you live."

"That you do." He extended his hand clasping the pink blossoms. "These are for you."

"Thank you, they're lovely." She brought the dozen buds up to her nose and inhaled the sweet fragrance.

Easton took a carafe from the wet bar and slid the flowers inside, pouring water into the makeshift vase. She was touched by the way he didn't order staff around to do his every task. He was a man with the money to pay for most anything he wanted and help for every moment of the day, and yet he lived a purposeful life.

He nodded to the flowers' placement before turning to her. "I thought about getting you candy too, but I keep seeing that basket full of edible toys back in that honeymoon suite."

Laughing, she pressed a hand to her lips and finally gave up holding back her amusement. "I'll return the vase once the peonies wilt."

She would be drying them as a keepsake for their baby. Far better to explain how she and her child's father had dated and enjoyed their time together. She couldn't bear for their child to feel like the unwanted result of an impulsive night.

Easton pulled out a chair for her at the wooden table. The peonies added the perfect touch to their romantic dinner, no one but the server and the musicians around.

Soft wind whispered as Easton pushed in her chair, his fingertips lingering for a moment on her bare shoulders. He took his seat across from her, foot knocking playfully into hers. His ready smile illuminated by the Tiki torch that kept bugs at bay.

Easton tucked his ankle against hers. "You really do look beautiful. If I didn't think to tell you before tonight, I apologize."

"You told me."

"You didn't believe me, though, did you? There's a skepticism in your eyes that stuns me."

Portia leaned closer to him, so her words didn't strain against the melody of the guitar and piano. "Of course I realize we're attracted to each other."

He touched her chin and tipped up her face. "You are lovely, elegant and always have been. It's all I can do to keep my hands to myself at work."

"You've always been completely professional in the workplace."

"I'm a damn good actor, then." He plucked a hibiscus from a nearby arrangement, spinning the stem between his fingers.

She laughed, unfolding her napkin and placing it in her lap. These luxurious meals were a treat, but she would have to watch her fish intake for the baby. Still, her mouth watered with hunger, a welcome relief from the morning sickness that grew worse each day. "I do appreciate and respect that you've been restrained in the office."

He tucked the flower behind her ear near the jeweled pin, ramping up her awareness. Distracting her from the parmesan-and-herb-spiced yellowfin tuna that overtook her plate.

"So it's okay for me to touch you outside the office now?"

"I didn't say that, exactly."

He dragged another flower up her arm, until it rested on her cheek. "I can see something's holding you back. Am I simply not your type?"

"Why do people assume they know my type?" She shimmied away from the flower, picking up her fork and skewering one of the roasted tomatoes.

"Someone else agrees with me?" He lifted one eyebrow.

"I didn't say that."

"I know I'm eccentric." Laughing, he pointed to the decorations overhead.

"You're brilliant and a gifted veterinarian who manages to work with a wide variety of exotic animals." Portia rested her fork along the upper edge of her plate. "And, yes, you're also one eccentric tree climb away from having your own television series."

"You don't make that sound like a compliment."

"I only meant I'm reserved. Some have even called me prim—" She held up a palm. "I'm alright with that description. I know myself. But you *are* eccentric. I would expect you to be drawn to someone more flamboyant."

"Some say opposites attract. I think it's more complex than that. Attraction defies reason."

So true. But that didn't stop reason from interfering with attraction, reminding her how hard she'd fought to be independent, to build a life for herself outside of her parents' shadow. She couldn't afford to forget that in the long term.

And yet, still, she burned for this man. Unable to resist for this one moment at least, she lifted her fingers to stroke his collar-length, wild hair. The touch happened before she thought better of it. And maybe it wasn't so bad as long as she knew it was her decision. She was in control. "Relationships are based on common interests."

"What are your interests? You draw, but what else?"

"I'm your secretary."

"My assistant." He corrected her gently, placing his hand on top of hers.

"Whatever. It wasn't your place to know my hobbies."

"We've spent more time together than some people do when officially dating. I should have listened better." He thumbed the inside of her palm, a small smile tugging at his mouth.

"Is this going to be round two of Quiz Show?"

"I was just going to ask you what song you would like for me to request from the pianist."

"Something with a beach music flavor. I love to dance."

"You do?" His bold mouth twitched in a crooked smile. "See, we have something in common after all. Hold on while I place our request."

He pushed out of his chair, heading to the pianist, all elaborate arm gestures and flash. An intoxicating vision.

Returning to the table, he extended his hand. "If you've finished with your dinner, could I have this dance?"

How could she resist? Right now, she couldn't. "I would like that, very much."

"I'm honored." He bowed deeply before whisking her onto her feet to the makeshift dance floor.

Pressing against each other, she felt time strain and stop for this moment. The scent of his cologne mingled with sea breeze and salt. He sang softly in her ear, his hot words warming her inside out.

His soft eyes met hers, desire and electric sparks passing through his gaze.

No matter what the future held for her, or how he reacted to her secret, there was only one way this night could end. Together, tangled.

Eight

Dancing with Portia set him ablaze. His hands had touched the bare skin of her back peeking out from behind her breezy green sundress. After the music faded, she looked at him through shy eyes.

"Walk me home?" her voice quiet, eyes burning into him.

Easton's hand trailed alongside her right arm, enjoying the softness of her skin, the way she seemed to melt under his touch.

He leaped at the chance to lace her fingers with his, for the extra time together. His stolen sidelong glances at her increased the farther away they walked from the main mansion to her modest off-white cabana. Her shoulders, normally strained, seemed relaxed. A light breeze tossed her half up, half down hair, the moonlight illuminating soft traces of makeup that accented her slender face and beautiful pink lips. She seemed like a tall fairy—an extension of the landscape. His landscape.

Their footfalls on the white sand road looked like shooting stars in the night.

Portia had always been naturally beautiful, but he couldn't recall a time when she'd seemed so at ease and calm. The spa afternoon had brushed life back into her, making it all too obvious to him how she always did things for other people and didn't do things for herself. He wanted to pamper her. He wanted to protect her. But as she spoke of common interests and viewpoints, he wondered if he should be protecting her from himself and his vagabond spirit.

She fiddled with her keys, fishing them out of her pale yellow purse. Shifting her weight from leg to leg, he noticed how her strappy sandals pushed against her skin.

The cabana she'd been given as part of her pay had been stark and basic when she'd arrived. Now the little wooden hut glistened with peace and beauty, her stamp everywhere. Flowers of nearly every hue overflowed from boxes and pots. Lush ground cover filled in spaces with only jeweled step stones breaking their flourish. A fountain built of terracotta clay pots overflowed into a pool of fat orange fish.

She unlocked the bright yellow door, brushing her feet on the mat before stepping inside and clicking on the lights. Inside, a plump, inviting sofa, in what he'd heard Maureen call a shabby chic print, nearly filled the room. There was an artistic flair to Portia he hadn't noticed before, in spite of her telling him she enjoyed drawing. He could see her creativity in the way she'd planned her garden and how she'd refinished old pieces of furniture, end tables with swirls of color patterned into the grain and shape. Even her simple ice cream parlor table sported handblown glass spheres that filled a bowl like crystallized treats. Somehow, he knew she'd made those, with her patience, frugality and eye for beauty. Why hadn't he thought before about how she commented on the distinct hues of the birds and other creatures in the wild?

And how had he not stepped inside here before now?

He'd missed so much about her until that night of the storm when he'd been drawn to her with new eyes, the electricity in the air gathering around her like lightning bugs. Even in trying to get her back into his bed, somehow he'd missed important details. Getting to know her had been a selfish plan, but he was finding himself more captivated than he'd ever been by another person.

"Portia, your place is lovely." Like her.

She slipped her shoes off and nudged them in line beside the door with her toe. "It's nothing compared to your professionally decorated mansion."

"You have an artist's flair to you that surpasses anyone else we could have hired."

"Thank you." A blush on her cheeks, she stared lovingly at her possessions. Proud of her space and vision. Confident.

"I like the way you brought nature inside." He stepped to the walls lined with pen-and-ink sketches of Florida coast scenery and animals. "And your art. These sketches are yours?" he asked even as he saw her initials precisely in the corner of each one.

"Yes, I mentioned I like to draw." She tapped one of her sketches, an alligator winding through marsh grass, a wry smile on her face. She'd never seemed so sexy, so decisive. So sure of herself as she was in the arena of her art.

"I remember. But this is more than just doodling or

drawing. This is talent, a gift." He turned back to her. "I respect the work you do for me. You keep me organized and focused in a way no one has managed before. But here, I feel like I'm keeping you from your true calling."

She looked at him thoughtfully, her love of art apparent on her face. "I'll get back to it one day as more than a hobby."

"Why one day? Plenty of college students work while enrolled. I did."

Taking his hand, she led him into the living room. She sat on the bright yellow couch in lotus position, patting the seat next to her. Inviting him closer. She leaned forward, interest and surprise knitting into her brow. "Even with your family's money?"

"Absolutely. I wanted hands-on experience." He sat too, linking fingers with her. Needing to touch her.

"That's nice to hear about you. I didn't know." Her palm rested on his knee in an unspoken promise of more to come.

This was another dance they were doing now, one he could see in the awareness in her eyes, the widening of her pupils.

"It must not have come up in your Quiz Show."

"I would have expected your life growing up, traveling the world, would have given you the opportunity for vast experiences."

"We were talking about you. And your brother. And why you refuse to let anyone help you with him," Easton said, not taking the bait to talk about himself. Portia so often deferred her interests and needs to others. He didn't want her to do that now. Not as he finally glimpsed her soul and her sparkle.

"Because I can take care of him. He's my family. He

has a learning disability. He's brilliant but needs tutors. He will graduate, it's just taking five years with summers. He's even picked up a part-time job as a residence hall advisor this fall. I'm proud of how hard he's worked."

"And then it will be your turn?" He reached for her cheek, stroking it with a soft thumb. Wanting to give her all of her dreams.

She placed her hand over his, stilling the motion of his fingers, yet pressing his touch more firmly against her skin. "I thought we were coming here to make love."

"Wow, I struck a nerve, didn't I?"

She rose from the couch, headed to the kitchen as if she were considering his words. Lingering by the fridge, she cocked her head to the side and popped her hip out. "Maybe I want to start getting hands-on experience with my art right now."

"What do you mean?" His heart pushed, hammered, at the suggestion in her pose, at her yet to be articulated promise. Standing, he strode into the kitchen.

"You can be my canvas." She pulled a tub of whipped cream from the refrigerator. She lifted the lid and swirled her finger through, painting her lips before licking them clean.

He almost swallowed his tongue.

She was distracting him on purpose. Of course she was. But looking at her right now, feeling the answering heat inside him, he would gladly let her. He would find out more about why she was delaying her schooling later.

After he explored every tasty inch of her. He couldn't take his eyes off her still-damp lips. "I assume that's my cue to get undressed."

"If you want." She shrugged nonchalantly, staring at him with a certain, commanding smile.

He made a mental note to make sure her future included all the spa days she wanted. Whatever magic Maureen had worked in getting Portia to take some downtime had paid off in spades. There was a new relaxation and confidence in her.

"I want. Very much." He stepped closer, unbuttoning his shirt and tossing it aside.

She swept her finger through the dessert topping again and touched his collarbone. Her stroke was cool from the cream, and then she dipped her head, her breath warm as she said, "Ooops, I need to erase that." She swept her tongue along his skin. "I'll need to draw that over again."

"Do I get to practice my artwork on you?"

"Are you any good?"

He took the tub from her and set it on the table by the colorful glass display. "I damn well hope so."

His hands damn near shaking, he reached behind her to unzip her dress until it slid from her body to pool around her feet. She kicked it to the side. He took in the vision of her peach-colored lace bra and panty set, her breasts perfect globes calling to his hands to explore. Her eyes held his as she released the front clasp. He was quick to help her stroke free of the scrap of lace so he could "paint" a snowy cloud of whipped cream over one nipple, lave it clean before giving equal attention to the other.

Her kittenish purrs of pleasure rewarded him for his diligent effort. She cupped his face and guided him back for a kiss. The sweet taste of sugar on her tongue went straight to his senses. Before he could gather his thoughts again, they'd both stripped away their clothes in a frenzy of motion on their way to kneeling on the kitchen rug.

Taking turns, they painted each other, although his

artwork was more precise than hers, Portia's more in the league of landscapes that sent her kisses all over. He focused more on her breasts, a trail down her stomach, then settled between her legs for an intense, intimate kiss. The sweetness of her had little to do with the topping and far more to do with her. Portia. This amazing woman who'd come into his life and shaken him from his superficial dating ways.

He wanted more from her. So much more.

With each stroke and circle of his tongue, her breathing grew faster. She gripped his shoulders, her nails digging half-moons into his flesh urging him to cover her body with his. He didn't hesitate.

He settled between her legs and positioned himself at the hot slick core of her. Something tugged at his mind but before he could finish the thought, Portia skimmed the arches of her feet along the backs of his calves and hooked her ankles around his waist. The arch of her hips welcomed him inside her. Where he belonged.

His head fell to rest against hers, the bliss of being joined with her so incredible it almost pushed him over the edge. He gritted his teeth to hold back his release, to make sure she found complete pleasure, everything he could give her before he indulged himself.

Stroke after stroke, thrust after thrust, he filled her and savored her rocking motion in sync with his. They were learning each other's bodies, specifics and needs, erogenous zones. The scent of her freshly perfumed skin and some kind of massage oils along her shoulders teased his every breath.

He would drink her in if he could.

Let her know how beautiful she was. Always. No makeover needed.

She was Portia. He'd not realized why he'd pursued her so stubbornly, but this surprising woman was who he'd been waiting for. And finally he was where he wanted to be.

That thought tore away the last vestige of his restraint and sent him hurtling over the edge into a blinding orgasm. His release sent him pulsing deeper into her, faster, each pump of his body drawing a "Yes, yes, yes" from her lips until... Her back arched upward. Her head fell back, her silken hair fanned around her.

No need for them to be quiet here in her home, just the two of them. Their cries of completion twined in the way their hands did over her head. Together.

His arms gave way and he just barely caught himself on his elbows before he rolled to his side, taking her with him. He folded her against his chest, their bodies sticky with sweat and the remnant of whipped topping.

In the stillness of this cabana, he felt at peace. The rise and fall of his chest made more comfortable by the press of Portia's body against his. His fingers stroked down her side. The moment of rest as beautiful as she was.

Easton kissed her cheek before nuzzling her with his late-day beard. "What brought on this change of heart?"

Portia looked up at him through long eyelashes. "Not a change of heart. I've always wanted this. I just felt like the time was right. This is our night."

"The first of many more, I hope."

She hummed in answer and kissed him, silencing any more talk or even rational thought, for that matter.

His hammering heartbeat started to recede into normal rhythms.

"We should get clean." He said into her skin. In response, she kissed him, deeply, her tongue darting over his.

"Done so soon?" She bit his bottom lip, hand wandering down his side.

She got up, her body a dark silhouette in the streaming moonlight. Walking to the bathroom, she looked seductively over her shoulder.

He wanted her, even more than before, and he planned to have her again and again. Thank goodness he'd brought enough condoms—

A sinking feeling slammed him in the gut. Damn, damn, damn it.

He was always careful. He'd only ever forgotten one other time, the first time he'd made love to Portia and when he hadn't heard anything from her in spite of his attempts to reach out, he'd known they'd somehow been lucky.

As he followed her toward the shower, though, he snagged his pants with his wallet full of condoms to use from here on out. They could talk about the lack of birth control during those other two encounters in the morning.

Because he wasn't letting anything interfere with this night in her bed.

Bright sunlight streamed into her room, nudging sleep from her eyes. Looking out the window, she began to turn her gaze inward. To memories of last night.

Allowing Easton to come to her space had been a big step. A bold one. Portia had allowed him to glimpse her private love affair with art—the one activity that steeled her nerves, made her feel brave and resourceful. She'd channeled that creative capacity into their night, blending art with love.

She stretched fully, remembering the way their tangled bodies sought each other as if by their own volition and inclinations. Portia painted him with whipped cream, made a masterpiece of his skin and her desire. Pulled him again into the shower. Needed him.

She'd felt like wildfire last night. A rush of flame and heat so intense, one that had to burn itself out. Which was where she felt like this morning was heading. To the aftermath. He'd used condoms those last two times. She hadn't wanted to break the mood by telling him it wasn't necessary, not when she already knew they would be talking about the baby soon, likely before her doctor visit. Because it wasn't fair to keep him in the dark now that they seemed to be heading into a relationship. Once she shared the news with him, things would change between them forever.

She turned from her side to see if he was awake.

Those bright blue eyes met hers, his dark hair curling on the pillow. "Last night was incredible. *You* are incredible." He stroked his fingers through her loosened hair. "I hope you don't run in the other direction again to put distance between us. Because I want us to be together. I want to see where this is going."

"I have no intention of running." She meant that. Running with their unborn child wasn't an option. She needed to face this head-on. No matter what. She'd been running from this conversation for too long.

"That's good to know." He leaned in to kiss her, then stroked the outline of her face. "I'm sorry for losing my head last night and forgetting to protect you."

"You mean not using a condom?" Bile churned in her stomach. The conversation was already headed in the wrong direction. She wasn't ready for this conversation. Not yet.

"Yes," he nodded. "That's twice I've let you down and

I'm sorry. But I want you to know that if there are consequences, I'll be here for you."

"Consequences." The word felt clinical. Distant. Emotionally shut off. But then she hadn't wanted the conversation to get emotional. So why was she bristling? God, her emotions were a mess and she knew it had more than to do with the baby.

"Consequences. As in pregnancy," he clarified. "Unless you're on the pill?"

All of her gusto and nerve manifested into steel will to cover the hurt his words caused. Part of her did want to rely on him and make a real relationship, but now she was second-guessing herself. Yes, she needed to tell him the truth. But she didn't need his help. Didn't need him to be obligated to her. Portia always figured things out on her own, made them work for her. Even if that path wasn't the easy or conventional one. "Don't worry about me."

"Of course I will. You don't need more responsibility on your plate in addition to your brother. In fact, can we talk again about me help—"

"No." She pressed her fingers to his mouth, surprised at the depth of her remorse over realizing they didn't feel the same way about last night. He was not ready to be emotionally involved with her, not ready to be a true parent. For a moment, she'd wanted to do all of this with him by her side, and she swallowed back the fantasy of being able to parent with him. "Can you stop talking about money and responsibilities and consequences? I know you don't want children. You've made that clear."

"As I recall, I said I don't think I'll be a good father and that I wasn't ready to start a family. Now that I think back I'm not sure exactly what I said." He scratched the back of his head. "You may have noticed but my thoughts get jumbled around you."

"You said you don't want children. I remember your words, and I would think a man of your education level would know what he's saying." Anger edged out her more tender emotions as she lobbed the words at him.

He reeled back under her attack, then he sat up, grasping her hand. "I'm not trying to pick a fight, Portia, although it's clear I've upset you. I'm sorry for that."

Portia tugged her hand from his. Distance. She had to put some space between them. And quell the rising tide of nausea building in her stomach. "Please, stop apologizing. I'm an adult. I'm equally responsible for what happens between us when we have sex."

"I'm trying to be honorable. Would you prefer I was a jerk?" His sincere blue eyes punctured her, calming her for a moment.

"Of course not." She shook her head, eyes stinging with unshed tears. The world pressed on her shoulders, pinning her to this moment.

"Then let me be a gentleman."

"Gentle is good."

The words stalled on her lips, heart growing heavy as nausea took over her body in full force.

He reached out to touch her, but she bolted from his fingertips. Running to the bathroom, door closing behind her.

Her bare thighs pressed into the tile floor as she held the porcelain toilet. Two types of illness bore upon her. One from the increasing intensity of morning sickness. That sickness she could manage—that one had an end in sight.

But her heartsickness over the lost chance to be with Easton in a real relationship?

She'd parented her brother and never felt this solitude—instead she'd taken comfort from her friends. Heaven knew she had friends and support here at the refuge.

Yet none of them were Easton. The abyss of her loneliness stretched in front of her as she heaved the contents of her stomach into the toilet.

Consequences.

The word sliced through her mind. She just wanted to curl up on the cool tile floor and not move for seven more months.

What was it about him that sent Portia running to lock herself away from him?

Easton sat on the edge of her bed, scanning the room. Everything seemed to have a definitive place. Bright, cheery colors served to accent the plain white walls. Her poppy-orange bedspread added warmth and comfort to the room.

She didn't have a lot of figurines or knickknacks, he noted. A small, skinny faux marble table sat in the corner, holding a bouquet of fresh-cut flowers.

Next to him on her nightstand, he noticed a small sketchbook, the spine worn from constant use. The visible signs of wear seemed at odds with the rest of Portia's room.

Glancing at the still-closed door, he decided to pick up the black leather-bound book. Leafing through the pages, he found himself transported.

Portia's floral sketches that hung in the hallway were beautiful. But the sketches in the notebook were stunning. Haunting, imbued with reality. She'd sketched different animals from the refuge, her images playing with shading and line structure.

He was no art aficionado, but Easton knew enough to realize Portia's raw talent. He felt a renewed dedication to getting her into an art program. She'd been self-taught. If she had resources, a mentor and time…she could be downright fantastic.

He replaced the sketchbook back on the nightstand, continuing his survey of the room. The top of her dresser housed a framed picture of her and Marshall, a gold-leafed copy of fairy tales and a ring dish where a pearl necklace coiled.

He picked up the book of fairy tales, reminding himself Portia needed her space. The door was still shut, but when they'd been at the inn, she had taken a bath and come out of that experience more relaxed.

Surely this morning was the same thing. He tried to convince himself of that.

But as time passed, seconds turning into minutes and then a full half hour without any sound other than the bathroom sink running and running, he began to worry. He hadn't heard the bathwater start, and he feared she was perhaps crying.

He walked toward the bathroom door and as he drew closer he realized…she was throwing up. Retching. Again and again. Worry overtook him and he knocked firmly on the door.

"Portia, let me help you. Do you have food poisoning?"

A long pause echoed, then he heard the sound of the sink turning off and the sound of what he thought was her head resting against the door panel.

"Easton, I don't have food poisoning. I have...*consequences.*"

Her words churned in his mind and settled. Hard.

He'd discussed the possibility of pregnancy with her but he'd been speaking hypothetically. This wasn't hypothetical. This was reality.

A baby.

His.

Inside her.

The sideswiped feeling stung along his skin much like a sunburn. But soon it eased enough for other feelings to flood through. Frustration that she hadn't told him before. That she had only decided to share it with him now that they were separated by a bathroom door and there was no way she could hide the pregnancy's effects. But at the forefront of all those thoughts? But at the forefront of all those emotions?

Possessiveness.

This child and Portia were now his responsibility. They were both officially a part of the Lourdes family circle. Given her independent streak, which was a mile wide, he could already envision her shutting him out.

He'd just figured out he wanted to create something real with her. No way in hell was he letting her walk away. He would keep her and their child, using whatever means necessary.

Nine

Portia pressed her head to the cool panel of the wooden bathroom door and waited for Easton's response to her poorly timed announcement. This was not what she'd envisioned when she organized the talking points for this conversation. She'd meant to roll out the pertinent details in a logical sequence. Warn him that she was prepared to take on this responsibility by herself. Assure him his child was in good hands with her.

Instead? She'd blurted out the truth in the harshest of terms possible.

Her heart pounded in her chest, slamming against her ribs that already ached from her extended bought of nausea. She could barely stay on her feet she felt so weak, a new low in her battle with pregnancy symptoms. She just wanted to crawl back in bed and hug her pillow until the birth.

With every day that passed, the morning sickness grew

worse. Although after today, she didn't know how it could be worse other than lasting all day long. Heaven forbid.

Should she call the doctor to move up her appointment date? Or…no. It was already Tuesday and her appointment was at the end of the week. Besides, she'd heard the old wives' tale that the worse the nausea the stronger the pregnancy. An upset stomach meant there were more hormones pumping through the system from her body's change. But she didn't have any scientific proof for that and couldn't risk her child based on internet articles.

She drew in deep breath after deep breath, wishing her little haven of a bathroom could be the place of peace it normally was. The old-fashioned claw foot tub had a Parisian-themed shower curtain hung from the ceiling, the whole room decorated in cream, mauve and gray. She'd painted a shadowesque chandelier on the wall with tiny rhinestone studs in the place of lightbulbs, a touch of whimsy that made her smile most days.

Rhinestones couldn't touch this nausea.

Hanging her head, her toes curled into the plush bath mat. She'd been so excited when she had come to the refuge and taken this job two years ago. The exotic locale had called to an adventurous side of herself she'd never indulged. This tiny house had been an unexpected bonus, a treat, a space to call her own since up to then she'd lived in Pensacola, close to her aunt's place, sharing an apartment with her brother. But the pay bump here had enabled her to head out on her own, and the timing had been right for her brother to spread his wings, too.

She had her own space, and now she needed to make the responsible choices that went with that freedom. Definitely she would give her doctor's office a call to see if her symptoms warranted an ER visit this weekend. They must have a twenty-four-hour service or a nurse on call to answer questions. She would not work over the weekend so she could take care of herself until that appointment on Monday. She would place the call as soon as she dealt with her baby's father on the other side of the door.

Heaven help her. She'd screwed up this announcement so badly.

"Portia?"

The low rumble of his voice pierced the bathroom door. She couldn't detect how he'd received her declaration about the baby. He'd told her he didn't want children...but the reality was, he was already a father. If he was half the man she thought he was, he would step up in some way. She'd seen him with his niece, and he was tender. Loving. She knew he would be as kind to his own child.

If she'd misjudged him, however, she could and would be a loving mother. She could take care of herself and her child. Her baby would be loved, not judged.

She swallowed hard, then took her time brushing her teeth, all the while bracing herself to face Easton. She splashed cold water on her face and toweled off.

Willing her hands to steady, she pulled open the door. Bright rays of sunshine washed over Easton, who stood, slightly disheveled, in crisp blue boxers.

Tugging on her oversized T-shirt, she really looked at him, taking in his muscled chest and abdomen. Sexy blue eyes filled with concern. His sleep-tousled hair perfectly accenting his sun-bronzed skin. Easton, the eccentric, wealthy doctor.

And the handsome father of her child.

What an exciting affair and romance they could have had if she'd only had the bravery to grasp this chance sooner. If she'd followed her instincts, which had shouted that they were both attracted to each other. Instead, she'd waited until it flamed out of control, and she had been too caught up in the moment to exercise her normal wealth of good sense. Knowing him better now, she wondered if his sense of honor had kept him from making the first move on an employee before the first storm that had brought them together.

"You're pregnant," he said, clasping her shoulders in broad, calloused hands. "With my baby."

"Yes." She resisted the urge to lean into him, to soak up the warmth of his body. "This isn't how I wanted to tell you, but yes, I am. Nearly two months along. I took seven pregnancy tests that first week I was so…stunned." Shocked. Scared. "They all came back positive. I called my doctor and she said to start prenatal vitamins, and we made an appointment for my first visit with an obstetrician. I go at the end of the week."

"Just a few days away." His voice was quiet, as if processing. He had to be feeling even more overwhelmed than she was. She'd had more time with the news.

She chewed on her lip before responding. "I was waiting until then to tell you."

"So you did plan to tell me," he said as he sat, causing fabric ripples on the bright comforter.

"Yes, God yes. Of course. What did you think I would do?" All she'd done was make plans since she had first discovered the news. Planned how to tell him. How to deal with a new addition to her family. She had a bullet list of baby needs. A monthly plan of action a mile long.

He shook his head, blinking rapidly, no words forming on his lips. After a small breath, he pressed on, "I wasn't thinking much of anything since I've had less than five minutes to absorb the news. I don't even know if you're planning to have the baby."

"I just said as much didn't I?" Heat built in her cheeks, hands growing numb.

"Not really." He grabbed her hand, studied her features. Her stomach gurgled an involuntary response and an aggressive wave of nausea threatened her again. "Portia? Are you okay?"

The scent of their lovemaking clung to the sheets. She wanted to crawl in the bed and press her head into her cool pillow and simply sleep the day away.

Another roll of nausea knocked into her along with a wave of dizziness. She fumbled for the edge of the mattress, gripping it.

Anchoring herself, she twisted the comforter in her fist. "Yes, I'm having my baby, and I plan on keeping him or her."

"My baby, too," he reminded her quietly, firmly. "I want you to put your feet up." Standing, he cleared a space for her on the bed, fluffing pillows before gently sliding his hands under her arms to prop her at one end. He also set an empty small trashcan nearby diplomatically. "In case you're feeling ill again, you can use this rather than getting up. Is this typical for how long your nausea is lasting each day?"

He went into doctor mode. She could see it in the patient way he asked her the question. Feel it in the touch he brushed on her forehead, surreptitiously checking to see if she ran a fever.

As his longtime assistant, she knew he was assessing her symptoms while trying to keep her at ease. Just like a sick deer. Or a surly monkey. How flattering.

"*Our* baby," she reminded him, remembering his possessive words. "And the nausea's gotten worse this week."

Her stomach churned again, bile rising in her throat. With a deep breath in, she tried to settle herself.

"Yes, ours, which gives me a say in the child's life." He took her wrist in one hand, his thumb squared over the pulse that she guessed was sporadic at best.

She felt like crap.

"I'm glad to hear you feel that way." She wanted to keep up her end of the conversation, tell him she didn't need his veterinarian care for her very human baby. Except she appreciated the way he tugged the blankets over her. Mopped a cloth on her forehead.

When had he gotten a damp cloth? Nerves pulled tighter inside her, making her head spin faster. She was glad he wanted to be a part of their child's life, but she could also feel her control of the situation slipping away.

"Portia, I would never abandon my child."

Determination and something Portia thought looked like hurt passed over his features, finding purchase in the tension of his expression.

"I know that." Yet while she knew Easton was kind, she hadn't been sure how he would respond to the news based on how quickly he'd bailed on old relationships. "Yet you've admitted to feeling ambivalent about parenthood. You've purposely steered clear of meaningful relationships and you climb around in trees like a mashup of Peter Pan and Tarzan."

"I'm not sure I like that analogy at all." He knelt in front of her, taking her hands in his, meeting her gaze with such earnest urgency in those mesmerizing blue depths. "But right now, the important thing is to make sure our child is healthy and thriving. Do you think you could hold down some water or ginger ale?"

She tried to answer but his concern for their baby— for her—touched her heart, and the more emotional she became, the more her stomach misbehaved. She was already so weak from morning sickness that she simply couldn't face another bout.

"I could try." She said it only to make the medical professional in him happy.

The thought of putting anything to her lips made her queasy. But this conversation was important in setting the tone for the rest of her and her baby's lives. She'd done such a poor job telling him about her pregnancy and now was her chance to set boundaries. Assure him she would be okay on her own.

Portia could hear Easton speaking, but the words grew softer as her head swirled. She worked to steady her focus by grounding herself in the beauty of his eyes, the rough velvet of his voice.

"Portia? Portia are you listening?"

"Yes, of course," she said softly, her vision growing fuzzy around the edges.

"Then what do you think?" he squeezed her hands.

He sounded so distant, fading by the moment.

"Easton?" She struggled to make sense of his words. "Think about what?"

Her fingertips seemed to lose contact with the comforter, sending her into a widening spiral. Nothing made sense. She tried to reach out for his hand. For the bed. For anything, really. But her vision sputtered, growing foggier as she tried to figure out what she thought about the proposal. No use.

More nausea, more dizziness, the room giving way like some scene out of *Alice in Wonderland*.

She fainted, her world swallowed by the unknown.

An hour later, sitting dumbstruck and numb in the ER waiting room, Easton stared hard at the window to the outside world as if he could somehow get himself and Portia back to that familiar reality. Not that staring helped. He barely registered the sway of palm trees or the glimpses of the ocean.

His thoughts kept turning inward, replaying the morning's events. Portia telling him she was pregnant, growing paler and disoriented. Portia fainting suddenly on her bed, scaring the living hell out of him.

Typically, Easton was the sort of man people liked to have around in emergencies.

When he was a teenager, he and his brother had hiked up a hill in Virginia. Their parents had let them have free range that afternoon. Easton had pushed them to explore. But as they neared the top of the hill, Xander lost his footing, tumbled down, falling on the rocks and trees, breaking his right arm in three places. Even then, Easton possessed a doctor's cool hand for dealing with injury and illness. He helped his brother to his feet, and calmly transported them both to a hospital. Fear never pushed at him once.

But today when Portia had been nonresponsive…he'd felt fear wrap icy hands around his heart and mind. The ride over to the hospital became a blur. She'd gone straight into a wheelchair, unable to stand without swaying. Seeing his beyond-competent Portia so incapacitated leveled him.

The staff's urgent and worried care revealed just how fragile and ragged she'd become. Why the hell hadn't he made sense of her symptoms earlier in the week? Maureen had told him something was off. He knew something was off.

And yet he'd ignored all those signs, too damn focused on his own goals. He was a first-class ass. By the time he'd handed her over to the hospital staff, her pale skin had felt so clammy.

The cackle of a loose parrot from outside snapped him back to the ER waiting room. He stood, wanting to be in the exam room with Portia. To do something, anything, to help her. Instead, he was out here. He sat back down, back pressing into the hard plastic of a lime-green chair. Across from him, he watched an older couple in their sixties talk in hushed tones.

The man's swollen ankle was propped up on a stool. His wife stroked his arm, love shining in her eyes along with a hint of irritation. Over what?

Not that it mattered. Easton just grasped for distractions.

Two seats away, a small girl cried intermittently. Her mom stroked her hair, cooed to her. Soothing the toddler. No father in sight.

Easton's heart seized. He wouldn't be that way with his child—an absentee father. If everything was okay.

Everything had to be okay.

Worry pushed into his thoughts again. He felt shock stiffen his joints. What if something terrible was happening to Portia right now? He clenched his hands into fists, squeezing. Trying to get a grip on the situation.

He'd been upset with her that she hadn't said anything to him before this morning. He wasn't sure what would happen with them. Her news had changed everything. But more than anything else, he wanted her to be okay.

A swoosh of the automatic doors sounded, letting in a blast of muggy heat from the outdoors an instant before a familiar voice called out to him.

Xander.

His brother had arrived, two cups of coffee in hand along with a bag of something.

"Easton? What's going on? I heard you were rushing Portia to the hospital."

"Who told you that?" Easton asked, surprised to see his brother huffing and puffing in front of him.

Xander snorted and passed over a large cup of aromatic java. "Do you think anything's a secret with all those volunteers around?" He held out the bag. "Want a doughnut?"

Clearly some things were secret since his brother made no mention of what ailed Portia. Still, Easton got the point. "No, thank you. The coffee's just what I need though. Thanks." He took a bracing drink of the nutty brew, then set the cup on his knee. "Portia's pregnant."

"What?" His brother blinked, surprise coloring his face. All that boardroom bravado gone. Xander dropped into a seat beside Easton, setting the bag and his coffee on the steel end table. "I'm...confused. Surprised. Details?"

"She's pregnant, and the baby's mine." Easton took another sip of the strong coffee. Too bad they didn't serve IV caffeine around this place.

"Congratulations, brother." Xander clapped him on the shoulder once, twice. "I assume you're happy—but hell, wait." Worry crept into his voice. "Why is she here?"

"Her morning sickness is out of control. They have her hooked up to IVs since she's dehydrated."

"All during the pregnancy with Rose, Terri battled that. You remember."

"Sort of, yes." A memory of his niece after Terri died

wandered across his mind. He'd taken her to the beach, built towering sandcastles for her. Easton told her stories of magical lands and talking animals. His flair for theatrics making her squeal with sharp giggles of uncontrollable laughter. He'd always thought his role as über-involved uncle would quell any parenting needs. Easton was crazy about his niece. But then Xander remarried Maureen and Rose didn't need him as much anymore.

For a few weeks, the lack of time with his niece had been strange. He felt like a castaway from that family unit.

But with Portia…

New possibilities leaped before him. He wanted Portia—he sincerely wanted to marry her. And he wanted to be there for their baby. To do whatever it took to be a good husband and father.

Because, damn it all, they would be a family. He wouldn't be relegated to the sidelines. He knew what it felt like to be an afterthought in his parents' lives. He wouldn't let his child entertain so much as a hint of a notion that that could be true.

He might not have planned on being a father, but he would figure out how to do this. He would be there for the baby and for Portia.

Xander angled forward, elbows on his knees. "You should be in there with her."

"They're going to let me join her soon. We're not married so I don't have a spouse's rights."

"You look shell-shocked."

"I only found out about the baby this morning." Easton combed his fingers through his hair, likely doing more harm than good. "I'm still…adjusting to the news."

Adjusting didn't even begin to cover it. He'd been set on romancing Portia, taking her out on dates, winning her back into his bed. He hadn't thought beyond that. He didn't do long-term relationships well. At all. His history spoke to that.

But now the baby—and yes, the power of his growing feelings for Portia—flipped his world upside down. He needed to think. To process. And figure out how to become someone she could depend on.

"Is she planning to have the baby?" Xander whispered, eyes darting around the emergency room.

"Yes, of course." He'd been so relieved when she had reassured him on that score. Of the million questions he had for her when he'd heard the news, that one had been the most important and she'd put his mind at ease.

"Then congratulations, brother. You're about to embark on the most amazing experience of your life." Xander slapped Easton's shoulders again.

"Thanks." He meant it. Still, he had worries and doubts.

His brother had embraced parenthood full-on. But he had always been better with personal relationships, too. He'd taken time to build something with Terri before they married and had Rose. Easton, on the other hand?

Every woman he had ever dated had been disappointed with his brand of interpersonal skills. Before, it hadn't bothered him. Much. But for Portia? He wanted to be better.

Xander leaned away, astute eyes locked on Easton. "You don't look happy."

"I'm just concerned about Portia right now." He wasn't ready to talk about his concerns and explain what a mess he'd made of things by not pursuing Portia outright after the tropical storm. He'd wanted her then, had played in his mind a million ways to angle for another night together, yet he had stopped short of acting on those thoughts. Now he wondered what had held him back. Whatever it was had made his life a helluva lot more complicated.

"Of course you're concerned about her and the baby. I understand. I'm sorry. What can I do?"

"I appreciate your coming here. You could have just called though, you know." He hated distracting his brother with personal matters. He didn't like burdening him or taking him away from his family.

"We're brothers. I was worried. You would have done the same thing if the positions were reversed."

"Truth." He nodded, meaning it all the way to his soul. His brother was his best friend, always had been. "You're right about that."

"And besides, you must have forgotten your damn phone again and didn't answer when I tried to reach you." Xander cast a sidelong glance his way, eyebrows knitting in faux annoyance.

Easton welcomed the ribbing, needing to share a laugh with his brother now more than ever. His laugh tangled up with his brother's, rumbling in the waiting room as a doctor in green scrubs stepped through one of the endless row of doors.

"Easton Lourdes?" the tall silver-haired doctor called, clipboard in hand.

Easton rose from his chair, lungs tight as he nodded.

The doctor waved a hand, motioning for him to follow. "You can see Ms. Soto now."

Portia kept her arm preternaturally still, glancing at the IV needle. Though she knew she could move her arm slightly, she felt like it needed to stay still as she processed the events of the morning.

She clenched her jaw as she looked at the ultrasound.

A tiny bean-like figure was displayed on the screen. Her baby. The future frightened her slightly—or it had until the doctor came in with the ultrasound monitor. She watched her child move, become real before her eyes.

Looking around the sterile white room, she knew she needed to plan. To figure out what direction she'd take. Her fingers itched for pen and paper...to make checklists and doodle storks.

The medicine she'd been given worked wonders. For the first time in weeks, she didn't feel sick to her stomach in the morning. That alone stabilized her.

The thin door that led from her room to the rest of the ER allowed muffled sounds to pass through the light wood. Sounds of machines beeping, a small child crying, a cart rattling down the hall. Adjusting her weight, the paper crackled beneath her, bringing her back to the stillness of her room.

The blue cotton hospital gown allowed air to kiss her back and neck, the coolness refreshing her as she leaned forward, letting her paper-shoed feet dangle off the edge. She tested her balance and found the floor didn't wobble or spin anymore.

At the sound of a quick knock, Portia raised her head and called, "Yes?"

"It's me." Easton's deep voice filtered through.

Nerves tingled but her stomach remained steady. She reached for the blanket and draped it over her shoulders and wrapped it around her protectively. "Yes, come in."

The door clicked open an instant before a wide hand swept back the privacy curtain. His broad shoulders and chest in a refuge-branded polo shirt filled her vision, blocking out the rest of the world. He shoved his hands in his jeans pockets. "How are you feeling?"

"Better, much better. The fluids help and they gave me something for nausea."

"So you're, um, both okay?" Concern furrowed deep in his brow, and for the first time since they'd met, he seemed unsure.

"Yes, we are." Lifting her left hand, she pointed to the ultrasound machine behind him. The image of the baby—*their* baby—was frozen in black and white on the screen. "You can see here. That bean is your child."

He turned to face the ultrasound machine, the profile of his face in her direct line of vision.

Portia watched the way his eyes squinted and refocused, almost as if his identity as a doctor disappeared, leaving behind a man in awe. Of course, she was aware he could read this ultrasound from a medical standpoint—note nuances, explain away the shape.

The man in front of her clearly did not process the image from such a technical angle. Instead, his lips, though pressed together, curled upward in a faint smile. His cheeks softened. She couldn't get over the expression of awe on his face. The possessiveness and pride etched into his stance. Looking at him now, she began to realize all his talk about not wanting to be a father was false or delusional. He'd already become attached. This baby wasn't just hers anymore.

And her baby's father was a man of money and power. She couldn't help but remember how his brother, Xander, had used that wealth and power to ensure he maintained full custody of his daughter after his first wife died. Portia had applauded his efforts, since in that case, his former in-laws had strange ideas about what a child needed to be happy.

But the incident worried her now as it occurred to her

Easton had the same kinds of resources at his disposal. He'd admitted he had never invested in a long-term relationship. What if he got tired of Portia but wanted more time with his child?

Easton eyed her, his rich dark hair falling in waves, catching the cold, sterile hospital room lights. "You're absolutely sure you're alright?"

"The hormones are really something else." She swiped away those worries, telling herself she was being ridiculous.

"Can I get you something to make you more comfortable?" He gestured around the room. He was trying, she could see that. "Like a pillow or another blanket?"

"Once the meds kick in a little more, how about an ice cream sundae, loaded with peanuts, bananas, cherries and fudge sauce?" Her taste buds shouted yes, but she still wasn't confident her stomach would cooperate. All the same, it felt good to dream that soon she could indulge all these cravings.

"Done. The freezer will be packed with options before we get home."

Home?

His home and hers were not in the same place, not really. Nothing was settled yet between them.

"I'm joking. Soon though, hopefully." She put her hand on her stomach, staring back to the ultrasound. To her future. "I just would like to have my simple, uncomplicated life back."

"That isn't going to happen."

"I know." She nodded, eyes drifting to the IV bag filled with fluid. Knowing that this was one of those defining moments—a moment she'd like to sketch or paint when she could.

"And I'm committed to being a part of my child's life." His voice carried such fierce determination, hinting at the kind of father he'd be.

The kind of father she *hoped* he would be.

"You're so good with Rose. You'll make a wonderful father. You're more prepared than I am."

He had a way of taking unexpected things in stride, a trait she'd always envied. His wanderlust soul necessitated quick readjustments. Portia felt like his personality prepared him differently for the trials of parenthood.

"I don't agree. You have brought up your brother. You help care for the animals. You have a great knack with the kids that come to visit the refuge. You'll be a great mom." He laced his fingers with hers, showing his sincerity in the strength of his touch. "But let me be clear, you won't have to parent alone. We'll be here for each other."

"So many details to work out." Her mind reeled. Now that he knew…well, she'd have to make all sorts of new plans. And backup plans.

"But we don't have to work them out now."

She chewed her bottom lip, confused. "How can we not?"

"Can you put the need for organization on hold for a while and let us live in the moment? We have months. Let's take things one step at a time."

"What's the first step?" She found comfort in breaking tasks into smaller portions, everything falling into neat categories and checkable boxes. She knew enough about Easton to know he didn't think so linearly. An intense curiosity burned in her as she waited for him to explain.

"First?" He stroked a thumb across the back of her hand before his blue eyes met hers. "Will you marry me, Portia? Make a real family for our child?"

Marry him?

Portia swallowed, an eternity passing between them. Words scattered from her mind, leaving her to only stare at him. What on earth was he thinking to jump into marriage so quickly? Sure, they appeared to be compatible, and maybe the relationship could go somewhere, but how could she know where for sure. They'd only had two dates!

Frustration bubbled up that he wasn't taking her concerns seriously. Their focus needed to be on parenting. Not romance. Not right now. She needed to protect her independence more than ever, for her child. Because heaven help her, she was starting to care for Easton—too much.

And didn't that thought cause the room to spin again?

"You're not going to pass out again are you?" he teased, tipping her chin up gently with one knuckle.

"No." She shook her head. Now more than ever, she needed her wits about her to withstand the will of Easton Lourdes. He might be eccentric, but he was a man accustomed to getting what he wanted. "I'm just not ready to make that kind of commitment. We have so much more to plan out."

"Fine, then. You're a planner. We'll plan." He stepped closer, wrapping his arms around her. "But just so we're clear, this time that you're taking to plan? I'm going to be using everything in my arsenal to convince you to marry me."

Ten

Two days later, deep, dark clouds encroached on the late-afternoon summer sky with threatening force. Tropical Storm Elliot rumbled in the distance, a menace that, if the forecasters were correct, would pass them by, turn into the Gulf of Mexico and eventually head toward Louisiana.

Sure, the outer bands of the storm would dump water on them with some degree of severity. But that weather shared more in common with a tropical depression—a resounding difference in destructive capacity.

Still, Easton wasn't taking any chances with the lives of the animals and people he cared about. He'd begun to organize the volunteer staff into small task forces—everyone charged with securing different aspects of the refuge. Just to be safe.

And, truth be told, he felt like he needed to keep busy while he waited for Portia to give him an answer about his proposal. Easton threw himself full force into storm preparations.

Hoisting a bag of bird seed onto his shoulders, he made his way around the atrium, opening the feeders with practiced ease. A brightly colored, talkative macaw cackled, landing on a tree limb overhead.

Easton poured the seed into the dispenser, his eyes trailing to the window where he saw volunteers scurry across the yard securing loose objects, checking shutters.

"Here we go," he said to himself. The macaw cocked its head, stretching wings wide and displaying the red underside.

"We go. We go. We go." The macaw's shrill voice made Easton laugh lightly.

"That's right. You sit tight during this storm," he told the bird as he made his way to the door of the atrium, surveying the flutter of wings. Antsy. All the animals were.

Then again, animals had a way of knowing things about storms that seemed to escape the notice of humans. Judging by their unease, Easton couldn't help but wonder if this storm would turn into something stronger than predicted. It'd been a few years since Key Largo had taken substantial storm damage, something he'd been incredibly thankful for. But as a Florida native, he knew that luck only lasted for so long.

Exiting the clinic, Easton noticed bright red hair against an increasingly gray backdrop. Maureen and his brother worked across the yard by the main mansion, checking the storm shutters. Rose bounced and waved from a navy blue carry pack on Xander's back. Her little blond curls rustled in the wind, streaming behind the toddler's face. Her expression lit up in a smile—too young to realize the severity of the situation.

His niece's peal of laughter carried on the wind, causing a wide grin to take over Easton's face. He felt it warming his eyes. She blew him a kiss, which he caught in the air. With theatrical flair, he pretended it took two hands to hold the kiss, wrestling with it. She clapped her hands, watching intently. Easton pulled his hands to his heart, patting lightly on his chest. Rose loved this game they played. He'd started this ritual a few days ago with her.

With the uncertainty brewing around the fate of his relationship with Portia, Easton felt desperate to fortify the connection with his niece.

Growing up, Xander and Easton had been well traveled, following his parents on adrenaline-fused adventures. Adventures that made him feel like the world had magic in it. When their father died in a mountain climbing accident, his mother had been like a ball that suddenly lost its tether. She skidded and skirted out of Easton's life. She'd simply checked out, a bohemian spirit that refused to settle. Another lost connection, another kick in the gut.

And Portia? Would he have to add her name to the list of the lost?

He didn't have the chance to dwell too long on that thought. There she was—barely released from the hospital, taking an active role in storm preparation. A protective desire stirred in him, drawing him to her. Making his way past volunteers carrying a kayak to one of the storage sheds, he approached her.

With the wind whipping violently, her hair loosed from her ponytail. She looked wild, fierce—a part of the stormscape. A force all her own.

She directed a group of volunteers carrying emergency supplies of water and canned food for the storm shelter.

He'd arrived by her side by the time the last member of the volunteer supply train had disappeared into the house.

Portia turned, knocking into him, her pointed features pensive but relaxed. Starting to walk, she held a clipboard in her right hand filled with a page-long checklist.

He loved that about her. *Loved?* The word caught him up short. He wasn't the kind of guy who thought that way emotionally, just that reason had ended more relationships than he could count.

He'd known Portia for two years—professionally, sure, but still a long time. Longer than most nonfamily relationships. He would have used words such as *liked*. *Adored. Admired.* But *loved*? He wasn't sure what to do with that word.

Easton shook off the tangent and said, "While you're deciding whether or not to marry me, let me help you."

"Help me?" She blinked at him, confused. She held up the clipboard as if to show him everything was under control.

He shook his head, holding up a hand. "Financially. You need to rest more. Put your feet up. Especially until you get the morning sickness under control. Let me pay for your brother's college and yours."

"Are you aware there's a storm brewing?" Her eyebrows shot heavenward with confusion. "I'm sure you have as much to do as I do. And furthermore…" She shook her head. "Why would you do that?"

"To ease your stress. I won't miss the money." Money was the least of his concerns. He wanted her well cared for. She worked so damn hard for everyone. She would never even think to put her needs first.

"You want to keep me closer because of the baby. You

want to put me in your debt." She met his gaze measure for measure, but her shift from foot to foot relayed her nerves.

"Of course I do. But I also want the chance for us to parent together. You and I both want what's best for all of us."

Her eyes narrowed, challenging him. "Don't play games."

Easton bristled, stopping in his tracks. He could be a lot of things—eccentric, stubborn. But he'd never been one to play games with people. He respected other living beings too much for that. "Think of the money as child support. This is what I should do, and it's what I want to do."

"You're not going to try to take the baby from me?"

The question shocked him silent for a moment. He'd proposed after all. He wanted to be a team. To tackle this together. "No. Hell, you're going to be an amazing mother. If anything, I'm worried about what kind of father I'll be. Surely you are too, after what I said about not wanting children."

Her eyebrows pinched together and she hung her head, watching their steps along the path as if thinking. "I've thought more about that, especially since our time in the emergency room, and I've decided you don't give yourself enough credit. I've seen you here with the animals. You have a tender, nurturing side to you whether you want to admit it or not."

Nurturing? "There's a difference between baby animals and human babies."

His words were practically lost to a roll of thunder. Rain, hard and determined, came pelting down on them. On instinct, his hand found hers and he gestured toward the barn on the far end of the property. She nodded in understanding, tucking the clipboard under her arm.

He pulled her forward in a brisk jog, making for the entrance of the teal-colored barn. Wind nipped at their backs, surprisingly chilly.

"How so?" she yelled as they picked up the pace, her fingers gripping his tightly.

He strained to hear her as they made their way to the barn. "There just is."

"Well, that's not very scientific," she said smartly. "I think nature kicks in either way."

And speaking of nature. He really needed to check on the animals in the barn, particularly the pregnant Key deer with a wounded hoof.

Around them, palm trees bowed to the ferocity of the wind, lightning sizzling around them like a sporadic camera flash.

They crossed the threshold into the barn. Portia closed the door, sealing out the weather.

"I'll check on Ginger Snap," she said, pressing a hand on his shoulder. He nodded, fumbling in his pocket to call his brother for a storm update.

Portia gave a small smile, heading to the pregnant deer they'd rescued a few weeks ago. Ginger Snap had a nasty cut on her right hind leg that he'd stitched. But before she could be released back to the wild, the deer needed to recuperate.

"Um… Easton?" Portia's voice interrupted his phone scrolling. He noted the urgency in her tone and jogged over to the stall door.

Ginger Snap was in labor.

"I think we're going to have to stay with her," Portia said, setting her clipboard down. No script for this.

Hell. She was right. He couldn't leave the injured deer, but his heart felt heavy. Conflicted. He wanted Portia to be in the safest place in the refuge. While the barn was up to current hurricane code, he would have felt better if she were in the storm shelter.

"Give me a second." He queued up Xander's number and pressed Call.

Two rings in and Xander's deep voice pulsed through the speakers.

"Where are you?" his older brother demanded.

"In the barn with Ginger Snap," he said, watching the deer pant heavily.

"You better stay there. Trees are falling. Debris is flying. Tropical Storm Elliot just got upgraded to Hurricane Elliot and it has turned to us. We're going to take a direct hit sometime in the next hour, brother."

Damn. The increased strength meant it was too risky to move Portia and her unborn baby.

"Thanks for the update. Stay in touch and stay safe."

Xander's voice sounded garbled. "You, too—" The connection winked out, lost to static.

"Are you ready for your first hurricane?" Easton asked, shoving his phone into his back jeans pocket as he turned to face Portia. Her face paled, eyes widening as she looked around the barn.

He pressed on. "We'll ride out the storm. We're in a safe place with plenty of supplies."

"If I didn't know you better, I would think you stirred up this storm to get me alone." Her lips twisted in a smile, spunk invigorating her. She looked at the office area in the barn—a small sofa, desk and bathroom. There certainly were worse places to be trapped. "I'm not sharing a bed with you just because we're trapped here."

"Of course you're not." He clapped a hand over his chest. "I'm going to be a total gentleman and give you the office sofa—since there isn't a bed here."

"You're being too nice. I'll feel bad if you sleep on the floor."

"I'm not going to be sleeping. There's a hurricane."

"Well, yes, there's a hurricane, so what exactly do you think you can do to hold that back? You're not a superhero."

"Good point. Although I guess I'll have to return my special hurricane cape."

A smile slipped between her teeth, then a giggle, followed by a full laugh as the tension eased from the room after their mad dash readying for the storm. Lord, he liked the sound of her laugh.

"That's better." He skimmed his hand along her arm, static easing back into the air again as awareness stirred. "You are right that we should both relax."

Her smile faded. "You make it so difficult to resist you."

He wished she didn't say that like it was such a bad thing. But he would work with what he could to persuade her. He sure as hell hoped nature would do its job for the deer. And for him and Portia.

Because the stakes were too high to consider failure.

Rain thumped and beat against the tin roof, the wind loud like the train Portia had ridden as a teenager when she went to live with her aunt. The breathy whistle of the wind felt unnatural—a sound that deeply unsettled Portia to her core.

For six hours, the storm raged, tossing debris into the metal-cased doors. It had made Ginger Snap's delivery stressful.

The tan deer's eyes had widened at the extreme noise, stress beyond labor pains visible in her deep brown eyes. So expressive.

But Easton had helped Ginger Snap. Spoke to her in calming tones, his voice seeming to have a mesmerizing effect on the doe. A beautiful fawn they'd named Cinnamon had been born about an hour ago.

So much excitement and stimulus over the last six hours had left Portia tired. She'd made sure to chug water, to stay hydrated. If she fell ill during the storm due to dehydration again, the options were limited. Her medication had been tucked away in the storm shelter. She felt fine though—and especially attentive to her body and her baby's health.

After she and Easton both washed in the small bathroom, bodies skirting and pressing against each other, they'd gathered an impromptu storm picnic. She ate like she hadn't in days, surprised by her own hunger.

Portia stretched out on a checkered blanket on the floor of the barn. Her body curved around the scattered snack plates—grapes, cheese, crackers. Easton stroked her hair, staring at the stall door.

She looked back at him. "I still can't believe I got to see that doe being born." The memory of the scene made her heart swell. Easton's practiced hands, his nurturing soul emerged in full force. Confirming what she already knew to be true about him. His parental instincts had been honed and developed by years of veterinarian care, his compassion ringing true.

"Cinnamon's a fighter. She's storm born. That's good luck and it means she's resilient." He smiled down at Portia, his tanned face warm and so blindingly handsome.

For a moment, she wondered if there was any truth

to the superstition about being born in a storm. Portia had been born in the middle of a blizzard. Good or bad?

Gathering her head into his lap, his hands massaged her shoulders. Invigorating her senses and soothing her unease about the storm. "How do you feel? Any troubles with the nausea?"

Portia leaned into his touch, his fingers releasing the ache in her muscles. Her eyes fluttered shut. "All's well. The food's amazing and the ginger ale really works. The midwife who stopped by before I left the hospital had some great suggestions. I wish I'd thought to reach out for help sooner."

"You don't have to do this alone. I'm here for you and our baby." He leaned close to her, folding his body to whisper in her ear.

"I do appreciate your saying that. And thank you for giving me space on the marriage proposal. I need time to adjust, we both do." It'd been two days since she'd been proposed to and hospitalized for extreme dehydration. Two days hadn't supplied her with enough time to make a life-altering commitment. She needed to weigh the pros and cons to arrive at the most logical course of action. She'd lived her whole life preparing to be independent. Now Easton was asking her to depend on him. She wasn't sure she knew how.

"The news is already spreading and I can't control other people's reactions."

The reactions of other people bothered her less and less. Her primary concern remained the health of her child. "Let's deal with one day at a time. For a free spirit, you're sure trying to think fifty steps ahead."

"Then let's focus on the moment," he said, pushing ever so slightly deeper into the knot in her right shoulder.

She melted into his touch, how his strong but intuitive hands knew just how to knead away the tension of the past two months. His thumbs found and worked loose a knot below her shoulder blade, then he stroked lower along her back.

And she knew—she just knew—she wanted, needed, more from this elemental moment alone with him. So beautiful in its secluded simplicity with the whole of nature at work around them, as tumultuous as her feelings for this man. She wasn't used to such a lack of control over her emotions, but right now, she reveled in it.

Angling nearer, Portia tipped her face up for a kiss, her emotions close to the surface after all they'd experienced together today. She palmed his chest, his heartbeat firm and accelerating against her touch. Her arms slid upward and around his neck, deepening the kiss, and with a hard groan he rolled her onto her back until they both stretched out on the quilt. The scent of the laundry detergent teased her nose along with the sweet musk of fresh hay. Clean and earthy and elemental all at once.

Easing her refuge-branded T-shirt off, she tossed it aside and met his eyes boldly, inviting. And as his eyes lit with fire, he didn't hesitate to unhook her bra and reveal her body to his hungry eyes. He stroked her skin, pulled away her shoes and jeans, touching and kissing and igniting her until her head thrashed on the thick quilt and she whispered pleas for him to get naked now, damn it.

A sigh of relief shuddered through him and he tossed away his clothes in a haphazard pile, his eyes staying linked with hers. Peering deep into her with fierceness.

Even in the muted glow of the barn's backup lights, she could still make out the definitions of his tanned, muscled body. Every fiber of her being screamed a possessive *mine*.

And yes, she saw how his eyes caressed all of her with clear appreciation, arousal. Desire. She'd never felt more beautiful, and truth be told, it had more to do with the way he touched her than with any look in his eyes.

Easton kissed along her neck to her ear, nibbling her earlobe and whispering, "Are you sure you feel okay? You were just in the hospital—"

Her fingers went to his sensual lips. "I'm fine, and the doctor cleared me for all activity short of bungee jumping."

"Well, then that's good for us since bungee jumping is nowhere on my agenda." He grazed kisses along her jawline back to her lips again. "But if you need to stop at any time, just say the word."

"Trust me, I will. Our baby means the world to me."

Easton's hand trailed down her side to her stomach, his eyes focused on her pale skin as he rested his hand there. A small, awestruck smile tugging at his mouth. "To me, as well."

Her heart softened at his words, and she reached for him, pulling him back over her, determined to take everything from this time together that she could.

The storm raged outside, but she and Easton were safe here together. But she knew too well the real world and worries couldn't stay at bay forever.

That marriage proposal still loomed between them, and she was no closer to feeling comfortable saying yes.

Sleep eluded him, but that was probably for the best. After they'd made love, they'd dressed and curled up on the blanket together. Portia fell asleep in an instant.

He wondered if his brother was safe or if the storm was letting up anytime soon. He'd tried to call Xander, but the cell phone reception was crap due to the storm.

They were in the oversize stall with Ginger Snap and her baby. It was the safest interior room in the barn. He watched as the deer tried to nurse her fawn, struggling to get the action right.

He picked up a piece of hay, rubbed it between his fingers and crooned softly, "You can do this, Ginger Snap. I know it's not easy, girl, but you can do it. You can be a good parent to your baby. You know what to do."

The momma deer flicked her ears toward Easton.

"I'm sorry we're not in the clinic, girl, but I'm here with you. Portia's here with you, too."

Oh Lord. Portia. He turned his gaze back to where she slept. Watched her chest rise and fall, the soft sounds of her steady breath reassuring him.

He could spend an eternity with her. And damn, but that rocked his world. And settled his footing all over again. He'd never found any woman he felt this way about, and he knew he never would again. She was... Portia.

His mind drifted back to their lovemaking and the spark between them. Incredible—like nothing he'd experienced before. He wanted to win her, to make her stay. Every moment without an answer to his proposal made him feel like she was a step closer to bolting out of his life forever.

Easton snapped the piece of hay, smiling at the deer. "And we care about you. You're not alone in this parenting. We won't let anything happen to you. We'll stay here with you all the way through. Although it's going to be a long night, I'm afraid. Care to answer? Because I could use some help on my end with being a parent."

Cinnamon started to nurse, which seemed to calm Ginger Snap. Her head rested on the barn floor as she appeared to relax, her stressed breathing becoming easier.

"You look like you don't even need my assistance right now after all. But then you deer have been having young on your own without the father around. So maybe you could tell me something about why Portia is being so stubborn about marrying me? Or hell, even talking about it?"

He watched Ginger Snap settle even more, her ears flicking attentively to Easton. The doe's eyes were deep and dark. But mostly, he noticed how calm she looked now. He tilted his head, laying a hand on the ground.

Portia stirred beside him, tossing slightly in her sleep.

He waited for her to settle before continuing, "Sure, you and she can do this on your own. But she doesn't have to. If she could just accept how much I care about her. I'm not going to leave her. I'm not like my parents. I'm steady. I've found a way to have adventures right here at home. I'm not...leaving..."

Portia moved restlessly again, stretching, then yawning as she woke. She sat up slowly, carefully, and smiled ever so slightly before pushing her tousled hair from her face. She removed a scrunchie from around her wrist and piled her hair high on her head. With bleary eyes, she reached for the water bottle, popped off the cap and took a sip.

Easton eyed her, worried. "Are you feeling alright?"

She took another sip, waited, then nodded. "All seems well." She picked up a cracker and nibbled it, as well. "Here's the real test though."

He moved closer, cautioning, "Take it slow."

"I will. Morning's close and I know what that usually means." She rolled her eyes and stayed still, waiting.

"No need to do anything other than rest." Damn crummy time for a hurricane. A sense of helplessness kicked over him even as he knew there was nothing he could do to battle Mother Nature's forces outside the barn door.

The winds sounded softer but he suspected that was merely the eye of the storm.

He stroked along her arm. "Have you given any more thought to my proposal?"

She held up the cracker in the muted light, scrutinizing it. She shook her head dismissively. "Can we talk about that later, please?"

Ginger Snap gave a huff.

"I know I said we had time to work on this during the pregnancy, but I'm wondering if that's a cop-out. We're good together. We've known each other for two years. We get along well, and the chemistry between us is incredible, beyond incredible. I've never felt this much for anyone else. Can you deny you feel the same?"

He meant it. Never had a relationship been more real to him. He'd ended other relationships quickly because he'd known they would not work out. He'd already spent more time with Portia than he had with any other woman. And even if he and she hadn't been romantically involved, he knew her.

Wanted her.

Couldn't let her go.

He wanted to provide for her. For their child. He knew he could make this work between them if she stayed and didn't bolt. How ironic was that? He'd been the king of leaving and now he could well be on the receiving end.

It scared the hell out of him. And also made him all the more determined.

"All of what you mentioned is good for dating or an affair. But it's not enough for a marriage." She set the cracker down, picked up the water again. Swirled it around as she stared at him.

"Why not?"

She put aside the water bottle. "Because it's not love. We can have everything in sync, all the chemistry in the world and without love, we won't last. That will be so much worse for our child. We have to get this right."

Ah, there it was. Portia's need for absolute perfection bubbling to the surface. That need had held her back in the past. It kept her from pursuing something if every aspect wasn't perfectly hammered down, all boxes checked. She'd waited for the perfect time to go to college too, but she'd been so busy planning, she'd never gotten around to just doing it.

"My mother and father loved each other and it didn't make them attentive parents," he snapped the truth, frustration growing. "Hell, they flat-out lost us in foreign countries more times than we can count. Most kids travel and learn words in other languages like *where's the bathroom* or *I'm hungry*. We learned *take me to the embassy.*"

She cupped his face in a gentle, caring hand. "Easton, I am so sorry. That had to have been terrifying for you and your brother and it's not right, not at all. But you also have to know that as much as you act like the absentminded doctor socially, when it comes to responsibility you are always one hundred percent there for your patients. You tell yourself you're an eccentric like your parents because that keeps you from risking your heart."

"Like you're using your brother's education as an excuse to keep from living your life?" he asked quietly.

"I'm taking care of him." Her lips went tight.

"He's an adult." Easton pointed out, reaching for her hand. "He can take care of himself. It's your turn to have a life. Marry me."

She snatched her hand away, anger brewing in her eyes, making him feel like the storm had jumped inside the barn. "I don't want to be your obligation and I don't want some marriage of convenience."

"My brother and Maureen married for convenience and it's worked out well for them. No one can deny that. Portia, I care about you."

"I realize that. You're a good man. But I don't want to depend on anyone. And if I did, it would be a man who loves me wholeheartedly. I deserve that."

"And you'll have everything as my wife."

"Everything?" Her head fell back in frustration and she sighed before she looked back at him. "You're missing the point altogether."

"And what is the point?"

"You've been thinking differently since you saw those glitter condoms in the honeymoon suite. Seriously. Glitter. Rubbers. Is that any reason to get married?" Scarlet hues rose high in her cheeks, anguish mounting in her voice.

Damage control. Easton needed to calm her. "The lack of condoms—glitter or otherwise—is how this happened. Plenty of people have gotten married for fewer reasons."

"This is not funny."

"Trust me, I'm not laughing."

"This is no way to start a life together. I don't even think I can continue to work here."

His temper rose, the weight of her words surprising him. "What the hell?"

"Don't swear at me!"

He pinched the bridge of his nose and closed his eyes. "I'm trying to figure out what's going on in that mind of yours."

"I'm the logical one. This makes perfect sense."

"Not from where I'm standing. Maybe it has something to do with pregnancy hormones—"

"Don't. Don't you dare suggest I'm illogical because I'm pregnant." Tears welled, hovering in the corners of her eyes even as those same eyes spit fire and back-off vibes. "I know how I feel and what I want from life. I want my child to be happy and I want to stand on my own two feet."

"We're both parents now. We need to make compromises."

"Oh, you really need to be quiet." She shot to her feet. Her voice reaching new heights, causing Ginger Snap to bleat. "I am not some kind of compromise. I will never be anyone's second-best disappointment ever again. I deserve better."

Head held high, she headed out. Hand on the barn's wide double door, she hesitated. Rain still came down in sheets, but the hurricane's eye could hold.

A massive crack sounded, like a tree splitting, and Easton bolted to his feet, racing to Portia. He snagged her in his arms and rolled under a low-lying support beam just as a falling tree pierced the barn.

Eleven

The barn warped beneath the weight of the tree, groaning—a sickening sound of metal buckling. A small hole opened like a wound, allowing a throaty chorus of hurricane force wind to enter the safe space of the barn and rain to drip on the floor.

Another groan. The tree sank lower, its branches scraping, cracking, filling the main part of the barn.

Portia wriggled beneath Easton, craning her head to look. In the wind whipping through the hole in the roof, he couldn't tell if she was injured or not. Her eyes were wide as she stared at the impending catastrophe a few feet away from where she lay pinned to the floor.

If the roof gave way. No. He corrected himself—*when* the roof gave way—she would be in the trajectory of the crash if he didn't get them out right now. He would have to worry about any possible bruises later. The situation was too urgent.

He pulled her close and rolled to the stall with Ginger Snap. His muscles screamed at him to move faster. He barely registered the unnatural coldness of the wind swirling inside, tearing at him, working against him. He tried to communicate with Portia, but his shout was lost to the roar and the howl.

Their fight didn't matter now. The only thing that mattered to Easton was keeping her safe. He kept moving, shielding Portia's soft body, pressing on through the invisible wall of wind filled with grit and twigs. Heaven forbid if a larger branch should come their way. He willed their bodies to move as one, shoving them both to the far left side, toward Ginger Snap and her newborn baby, who cowered in the corner. The two deer cried and bleated in unison, fear rampant in those deep, dark, knowing eyes.

Finally, Easton found a solid wall under a reinforced steel beam, the other corner of the stall and the reason he'd chosen this spot in the first place. He pressed Portia against the wooden planks of the side, rain drifting in through the branches and pooling on the floor. Rain still hammered outside, beating the roof and the ground. He kept his back to the storm just as the tree crashed the rest of the way into the barn. Sliced the metal clear open as wind and sky flooded them with the unnatural sounds of raw power.

Thick, sideways rain pelted inside, and the shifting tree brought a scream from Portia. He hugged her closer. The oak moved one last time, settling, in a surreal way almost sealing off the elements beyond.

For now.

Heart hammering in his chest, Easton's body pressed against hers. He counted them lucky to have been out of the fall zone of the tree.

Easton felt her inhale sharply, holding her breath for a long time. Noted the ragged pace of her heart as she loosed the breath. The release of air seemed to rival the strength of the storm.

She leaned into him. To Easton, it seemed as though her body might melt into his. He felt the tension in her stance, the fear in her skin. Despite the near-deadly experience, he felt strangely calm as her light floral perfume wafted by him. A glimpse of normalcy.

How he wanted to protect her against all threats and hardships. Weather. Health. Finances. All of it.

Portia's messy ponytail tickled his nose, reminding him of gentler times with this sexy woman. Of being in a bed—a true bed with her.

He inhaled deeply, steeling himself against the pelting rain as he dared a look behind him to survey the damage.

The structure of the barn was intact—they wouldn't have to demolish the building. But the barn had received substantial damage from Hurricane Elliot.

But all of that could wait. Portia softened beneath his touch. She reached her slender hand for his, entwining their fingers. He squeezed tightly and then dropped her hand. Thunder and wind assaulted their senses, but they were close enough for Easton to reassure his pounding heart that Portia hadn't been hurt.

In a bellowing voice while checking her over with careful hands, Easton asked, "Are you alright?"

"Yes, yes, I'm fine." She wriggled under him. "More importantly, how are you? You're the one who put himself in harm's way."

"Not a mark on me. But I need to secure that area where the tree came in with some tarps or the whole place could flood by the time the hurricane passes."

He looked back over his shoulder, mentally planning and strategizing what needed to happen.

She chewed on her lip, eyes trailing to the damage. With a vigorous shake of her head, she pressed up. "I'll help."

A snort escaped him before he thought better of it. He appreciated her resilience, her willingness to pitch in and help out. But being knocked around by hurricane-force winds and soaking to the bone? Not an option. "Like hell. Be still and try to stay calm for your sake and for our baby. I don't want you doing anything until you've been checked over."

Her spine went straight and rigid. "I'm careful."

His jaw went tight and he couldn't resist snapping. "Careful? Like when you tried to run out into a hurricane?"

Her eyes filled with tears, and she pressed a hand to her mouth. "You're right. I wasn't thinking. Oh God, how could I have been so reckless?"

His anger dimmed in the face of her tears, and heaven knew, he didn't want to upset her more.

He clasped her fingers, trying to soothe her. "And that's why, for the baby's sake, I'm sure you'll sit over there and watch Ginger Snap and Cinnamon. We can argue until we're both soaked or you can let me get to work."

She nodded, a mixture of annoyance and defeat in the thin line her lips formed. But she didn't argue. Instead, she grabbed the quilt from the floor and walked slowly to the deer, hands extended.

Easton heard her talk to the deer. Reassuring them everything would be alright. She sat in the hay next to them, eyes fixed on the fawn.

Easton moved quickly to the small office, grabbing

a tarp from the supply closet. Scouring the shelves, he located nails and a hammer from behind a stack of toilet paper.

Knowing that he didn't have much time to make an effective barrier, his limbs sang to life. He hammered a tarp wall, reminding himself the entire time that he needed to make sure Portia stayed safe. He wouldn't have her catching her death out here.

With the help of a ladder and some rope, he got to work, using the grommets on the tarp to stretch it in some places and using nails to secure it in others. In a few places, he nailed the thing to the fallen tree, but in the end, he did a decent job protecting them from the rain.

The blue tarp wall wasn't going to win him any construction awards, but as he stepped back to survey his handiwork, he knew it'd do its job. Nothing more, nothing less.

Putting away his tools, Easton found a clean T-shirt in the barn office. He toweled off his head and walked back to the stall where he'd left Portia and the deer. He stopped in his tracks.

Like some woodland fairy, Portia was wrapped in a quilt, fast asleep. Her head cradled by her arm, which rested on Ginger Snap's rump with Cinnamon curled between them.

She'd been wiped out. That much was clear.

But something else gnawed at his consciousness as he looked at the strange scene in front of him.

For the last several years, he'd been convinced that because Terri and Xander had joined the efforts of the refuge and set up shop here that he'd been at the core of a family. He'd been more convinced after Terri passed away, leaving Easton to help with baby Rose.

He was happy here, sure. He'd enjoyed the rewards and benefits of a family without any of the investment or risk. That'd been his role.

But as he stared at Portia, watched her sleep nestled up next to a deer, he began to realize that wasn't the role he wanted. He'd been playing it safe for too long, keeping his relationships light and easy until he'd reached this point where he didn't even know how to have a deep and meaningful one. All that was about to change, however. Because Easton didn't want a sideline role anymore. He wanted something lasting, with the strong, sweetly fierce woman in front of him.

This Peter Pan wannabe was ready to leave Neverland. To follow his Wendy.

He didn't just care about Portia. He loved her.

Marrying her wasn't about the baby. It was about building a life with her, forever. And he'd sabotaged his proposal by not recognizing her most vulnerable of insecurities. He'd made her feel like an obligation rather than a precious treasure.

No wonder she'd tried to storm out of here.

He'd minced his words, convinced her that their circumstance as parents were the reason he'd wanted to pursue a relationship with her.

That formulation had been completely wrong. He loved her enthusiasm for logic and how that balanced her artistic soul. Easton loved the way they balanced each other. His love for her coursed through his veins. He didn't know why he hadn't recognized it before.

He loved her. Not for her secretarial skills. Not as a valuable employee. He loved Portia for all that she was—sacrificing, kind, artsy and wildly sexy. All of her.

Now he had to persuade her to say yes.

* * *

So after a crash in the barn and another five hours trapped in said barn, Portia had weathered her first Category 3 hurricane. Now, in the strangely bright morning sun, she sat on a kitchen barstool watching the cleanup effort through an open window, cooled by a fan running off a generator. She should have gone to the doctor by now, but that had been rescheduled due to the storm.

Both Easton and Xander refused to let her help. The ER scare and the stress of the storm had them both convinced she needed to rest. To stay away from any form of physical labor.

So here she sat on a stool in the kitchen looking out the window. And looking. And looking. Just as she'd been stuck in the barn unable to act. Sure, she'd slept. But even when she was awake, Easton wouldn't talk to her or let her exert herself in any way, physically or emotionally. As if her emotions weren't already in a turmoil regardless. Thank goodness one of the volunteers was a nurse and had checked her out or she would be in an overrun ER right now. And Portia had to admit to a massive sense of relief that Easton and their baby were okay.

And thank heaven there were no casualties, human or animal. All damage had been structural, which could be repaired with time.

She propped her chin on her elbow. She felt like a true Floridian now, down to a leveled house. Her small white cabana hadn't been a match for Elliot's relentless winds and storm surge. The majority of her belongings were probably floating to a distant shore, displaced.

Like she felt. Out of sorts.

At least not everything had been lost. Some photo albums and sketchbooks she'd tucked away in her closet remained. Some clothes, too. But there was so much damage.

Every line of sight and perspective revealed more destruction. Debris littered the lawn, pieces of people's lives from yards away. A Jet Ski, pieces of a dock, even a window air-conditioning unit. She could barely see the presence of light green grass.

She'd been through snowstorms before, when traveling with her parents, but there was a crystallized beauty after a blizzard. People holed up with hot cocoa in front of the fire. This kind of destruction and loss after the hurricane humbled her. Made her feel small and fragile. Made her question her need not to rely on anyone.

But so did being confined to the main house while other people worked to make the place habitable again. Volunteers picked up debris, moving branches and pieces of buildings with military precision. Or, she thought, a laugh pushing at her lips, with ant-like precision—moving things so much larger than the human body.

Maureen kept Portia company, pouring her a glass of water. Maureen's red curls fell in her face, making her look wild. "Anything else for you, love?"

Picking up the orange-tinted glass, Portia shook her head. "Not unless you can sneak me outside so I can be useful to somebody."

Maureen put a hand on Portia's shoulder, shaking her head. "Everyone just wants to make sure you are okay. And you are being useful. Honestly. Taking care of yourself is useful to all of us. We care about you, you know."

Portia had grown to appreciate her friend's blunt honesty. She simply nodded.

From across the kitchen counter, Portia's phone rang, vibrating like mad.

Maureen glanced at the caller ID. "It's your brother. I'll leave you to it." She gave Portia a side hug before disappearing into the house, her footfalls echoing until they were silent.

She slid over to answer the phone, steadying herself.

"I've been so worried about you," Marshall said by way of greeting.

Portia traced the ridge of the glass with a light fingertip, staring nowhere in particular. "Well, hello to you, too."

"I feel like when one sibling goes through a crazy hurricane unexpectedly, hello falls a bit short. Are you okay?"

Was she okay? Again, she didn't know how to answer that.

"Of course I am. I'm not going to lie, Marshmallow. The hurricane was the most intense thing I've ever witnessed. But I am okay. Everything here is just fine."

"You just…" Marshall trailed off. "You just don't sound like yourself. I can come see you, take a job in Key Largo and help you out."

The words knifed Portia in the chest.

"Absolutely not." Portia took a sip of her water, deciding not to tell him about her destroyed cabana. He didn't need to be worried by that. Hell, that would send him on a plane within the hour.

She pressed on. "Finish school and then kick butt. That's what would make me happiest."

He paused, sighing. "Fine. But I'm coming to see you this weekend."

She stuttered. "That's really un—"

He interrupted her. "No, it is necessary."

"Okay," she found herself saying. "Yes, please. I would like to see you. I, um, need to see you. I've missed you."

"I miss you, too. See you soon, sis. Love you."

Portia looked back outside at the chaos. "Love you, too."

He hung up, leaving Portia to her swirling thoughts about letting others into her life, accepting help and comfort. She couldn't hide from the truth. She needed other people as much as they needed her.

The realization settled inside her with a depth that went beyond just the physical implications of a hurricane, and made her question all the times she'd pushed offers of help away. She'd denied people the chance to give back the way she gave to others.

And why?

To protect herself from rejection? To give herself control over her world after a tumultuous childhood? Maybe. Probably. The whys didn't matter so much. What mattered was changing, becoming less rigid in her views and broadening her scope, letting love into her life as well as giving it.

She saw Easton from a distance. She would know his walk, his stance anywhere, even if he wore a tuxedo rather than his regular cargo pants, boots and T-shirt. Or nothing at all. Her heart squeezed with emotion.

She couldn't hide from the truth anymore. She'd fallen totally and irrevocably in love with him. Chances were, she'd loved him for a very long time and hadn't allowed herself to admit it to herself because her feelings weren't logical.

Love wasn't logical. It wasn't based on looks. Or a checklist. Or criteria. Feelings couldn't be stacked into a neat, orderly pile. Her emotions were messy and tangled and to hell with independence.

Her soul hurt so much because she loved him, completely and irrationally. Her feelings didn't make sense and they weren't supposed to. This was about leading with her heart rather than her brain. She'd worked so hard not to be like her mother, Portia had missed the whole point. Her mother hadn't really loved anyone but herself. All of her mother's relationships were based on—checklists and criteria. Portia may not have looked like her mother, but in a sad way, she'd fallen into the same trap.

How sad was that? Tragic actually.

Hopefully she wasn't too late to change things and build a future with Easton and their baby. A future built on love.

As Easton drew nearer, he caught her stare through the window. In his arms, he carried stacks of her artwork. He raised them above his head, a smile forming on his face.

But not on hers. She knew this gesture was a kind of peace offering, and oh how she wanted to accept it. But sadness blanketed her, pulling her heart into a plummet.

Because as deeply, completely and passionately as she loved him, she now understood her own self-worth.

She'd always wanted to be independent. Well, this was her test. She owed it to herself and to her child to stand up for herself. As soon as the cleanup was completed, she would demand the fullhearted commitment from Easton they all deserved.

A week later, fading sunlight washed the bruised but recovering refuge in orange hues. As Easton scanned the outside patio tables, he could barely believe that a week ago, the place had been torn apart by Hurricane Elliot.

The substantial damage to the barn and clinic had been repaired. Both Xander and Easton spared no expense, contracting the quickest, best construction companies in southwest Florida to bring the structures back up to tip-top shape.

As he looked around the gala fund-raiser tonight, he could see all of that hastened hard work paying off. Manicured grass, well-maintained buildings. Normalcy.

Which was exactly what he needed to show the collection of celebrities, politicians and socialites that bustled from table to table with champagne glasses in hand.

A snazzy pianist set up on a pop-up wooden dance floor, string lights winking on overhead, creating an illusion of stars brought down to earth. The pianist's notes mingled with the jazz singer whose sultry alto voice spit out lyrics from crooners of another more elegant age.

The brothers had agreed this event would be black-tie and impressive. They needed to be out in public view to fully demonstrate their success as an organization for the reopening of the refuge. So the Lourdes brothers had pooled their connections, hired a decorator and thrown a major event together in five days' time. Impressive, even for them.

As he watched the black-tie affair unfold in his backyard, Easton felt proud of the roots he'd laid down here. The roots he hoped to add to tonight.

The Serenade to Starlight signified the official reopening of the wildlife refuge. This event allowed them to renew their presence in the public eye, something completely essential for maintaining their facilities and the care of the animals.

The whole place seemed to twinkle in cool silver lights and accent pieces. The guest list consisted of A-list types from Miami, South Florida and the Keys. A few prominent West Coast starlets had flown in as well, lured by the promise of positive press coverage for their philanthropic efforts. Of course, the brothers made sure the volunteers could attend, too. The refuge depended on their time, effort and grit. They deserved to enjoy this evening.

Still, a moment of pride and joy turned to apprehension as Easton scanned the crowd, zipping past the women in cocktail dresses. Skipping over the heads of the politicians with cigars and whiskeys on the rocks. He spotted Maureen facilitating media coverage. Xander shaking hands with one of their big donors.

There was only one person is this crowd of people he really wanted to see, however. And that was Portia.

Since the storm, they hadn't had a moment alone. Despite living in the mansion together—under the same roof—she'd kept her distance. Their conversations had been short, quiet. An air of pensive distraction painted her face and actions all week, but he'd wanted to give her time to collect her thoughts and recover from the storm.

Some time where he wasn't pressuring her about marriage.

And she'd retreated totally.

A lesser man, one not dedicated to wooing the love of his life, might have turned tail and given up. But Easton had never been that kind of man. His bones didn't allow him to quit. He knew when to use his theatrical, eccentric, romantic heart. He'd laid down a plan to win her over. Moreover, he'd determined a way to prove how important she was to him.

Then, he spied her through the crowd.

His heart hammered, breath catching in his throat.

Portia rested a slender hand on one of the cocktail tables set up by the massive pool. Her hair was piled on her head, but not in her normal ponytail. Instead, her hazelnut hair was swept into an Audrey Hepburn bun. A slinky peach ball gown clung to her curves, suggesting her natural grace.

Damn. She was sexy.

She moved and the peach-colored dress shimmered in the lights as she leaned to talk to her brother, Marshall, who'd decided to visit for a week. That was another reason Easton had wanted to give Portia space. He knew she needed to spend time with her brother.

But tonight, it was Easton's turn. And he had to get to her.

His brother clapped him on the shoulder, a small glass of bourbon neat in his opposite hand. Easton's open stare at Portia interrupted, he turned to face his brother.

Xander winked at him, understanding what was going on.

Jessie flanked Xander, a vision in glittering silver sequins. She absently straightened Don's bow tie as she spoke. "You boys have completely outdone yourselves."

Sipping his bourbon before answering, Xander nodded. "We just wanted to express our appreciation for the hard work of the volunteers."

"We wouldn't be here without all of you," Easton added, his eyes watching the governor. A few feet away, the man paused. He stooped down, a smile on his wide, tanned face as he took a bright pink carnation that Rose offered him. She clapped when the governor stuck the flower behind his ear. Rose waved goodbye to the official when Maureen scooped her up, heading toward her husband.

Rose's bright eyes lit up when she noticed Easton. She bounced in her sunset-yellow smock dress, blond curls catching in the light summer breeze, twisting over the green wreath crown in her hair.

Rose looked over at her uncle and blew a kiss. Easton caught it in the air and pressed it into his heart. And in that moment he knew he would continue the ritual with his own daughter one day. Because yes, while he couldn't explain why, he knew without question that his and Portia's child was a girl.

A daughter. A son would be great, too. But he already could envision his and Portia's little girl in his heart's eye. And she was incredible.

The pianist and jazz singer faded, their set coming to an end. Elle Viento, a famous singer-songwriter, was up next. The brothers had flown her in from her vacation house in Destin, Florida, to sing.

Her guitar and soft vocals rippled through the crowd, giving the guests a small pause. Even Harvey Fink the movie star stopped to watch Elle play.

The gorgeous night needed to stay this way. Just a bit longer. Just until Easton could make his way to Portia.

Don interrupted Easton's thoughts. "I'll bring you another drink, dear," he told his wife, kissing her on the cheek before disappearing to the bar. Jessie looked like a schoolgirl, her eyes glowing.

"So, Easton, how is Portia? Things settling between you two?" Jessie asked in her matter-of-fact way.

He exchanged a glance with Maureen. "She's fine. And we're pregnant."

Easton wasn't concerned with hiding that truth. He loved Portia, and didn't care who knew what anymore. All that mattered was proving himself to her.

Jessie's hand went to her chest, eyes wide. "Pregnant?" Her tone questioning, prying.

Maureen nodded, saving Easton from answering every single nosy question. "Yes and she is doing well. Glowing and excited."

But Easton wasn't going to let Jessie think he needed shielding from the invasive questions. He was more than ready to declare himself.

"And I have every intention of romancing her for a very, very long time. I love that woman." Every fiber of his being sung that revelation.

Maureen's grin spread like wildfire to Xander and Jessie. She playfully shoved his arm. "Now, there's the magic word. Go get her, Doctor."

Easton winked, setting out to find Portia. He strode over to her, resting a hand on the cocktail table.

Marshall welcomed Easton with a big, toothy grin. The young man's square features contrasting with Portia's slender, angled ones. The sibling resemblance came in their slender height and inquisitive brown eyes. Easton had learned to size people up quickly after all the moving around he'd done in his childhood, and Marshall was a good kid, really bright. Easton understood why Portia sacrificed so much for him.

Easton cupped Marshall's shoulder.

"Do you mind if I steal your sister for a while?"

Marshall smiled, but pinned Easton with a serious look far beyond his years. "As long as you take good care of her."

"I promise, on my honor." He thrust out his hand for the young man to shake. He hoped Marshall would soon be his brother if all went according to plan.

Marshall nodded, his dirty blond hair flopping on his forehead. He turned his attention to a young soap opera star in a bright green dress with a vee neck open to her navel.

Laughing, Easton turned away, focusing his full attention on the only woman at this event who mattered to him. Portia. He ducked his head to whisper in her ear. "I think it's time we talk."

"Right now?" She glanced up at him, her eyes scanning his as if she were looking for something.

"We've put it off long enough, don't you think?" He touched her elbow. "Come on, I have something in the barn I would really like you to see."

She chewed her glossy bottom lip for an instant before nodding. "Yes, of course. I'd thought perhaps we should talk after the property cleanup and celebration, but there's no need delaying."

He took her hand in his, leading them beneath the twinkling paper lanterns toward the barn. The rustle of music and cocktail conversation faded the closer they got to the newly rebuilt structure, repainted teal just like the old one.

Easton placed his hands over Portia's eyes. "No peeking," he teased, nudging the door open with his foot.

They crossed the threshold, lights activated by their movement.

"And now." He took his hands back, letting her see the barn.

Framed pieces of her salvaged art work decorated the barn. Some paintings hung from the rafters and were surrounded with shimmery lights. Billowing flower stalks in sunset-colored pots lined the barn, leading toward a stall at the end of the row.

Ginger Snap poked her head out, ears moving. Portia stepped forward, eyes going from piece to piece and then to the fawn Cinnamon who stood tall beside her mother on spindly legs.

Atop a pile of fresh hay, Easton had laid a brilliant white-and-gold quilt at the far end of the barn. Then he'd covered the blanket with a tray of bright, tropical fruit and crackers. Two champagne glasses flanked an ornate bottle of sparkling water.

Easels lined the path to the blanket. He took her hand, led her to the picnic.

Bright pink calligraphy scrawled across the first canvas: You're Beautiful.

She moved on to the second, a smile lighting her eyes as brightly as the strands of twinkling bulbs illuminating the barn: You Drive Me Crazy—And I Like it.

At the next canvas, her fingers went to her lips, her gaze wide: Easton Loves Portia More Than Life.

Her hand slid away from her mouth, her fingers trembling as she traced the two words on the final message: Marry me.

Tears filled her eyes, one, then another sliding down her cheeks.

"Hormones?" he asked.

"So much more," she answered. "Easton, you are…so charming. And so ridiculously handsome."

Delicate hands stroked his tuxedo lapel, moved to his face. His heart was barely contained in his chest as he looked at her, reading the supreme tug of emotions in her eyes.

He needed that emotion to be love. His whole soul sang his love for her. If she left…he couldn't even finish the thought. Her absence would devastate him.

Easton dropped to one knee and pulled out a ring box

from his back pocket. He popped it open, letting the lights bring the solitaire diamond to life.

Portia's hands went to her mouth, tears streaming down her face.

"I love you. I never thought I would find a woman who would make me want to settle down and figure out how to really be in a relationship. But then I met you and everything changed. Portia, you are the kindest, most self-sacrificing person I've ever known. I want to spend the rest of my life deserving you. Will you marry me?"

She clasped her hands to her chest. "Yes. Yes. Yes, Easton."

Relief swept away the buzz of nervousness he'd refused to acknowledge until that moment.

He stood up sweeping her into a hug, kissing her deeply.

"I love you so much, too." She said as he slipped the ring onto her finger. A perfect fit—as they were for each other.

"No worries about me being Peter Pan and Tarzan combined?" he half joked, unable to keep from worrying. He needed her to believe in him.

"I'm thinking I may have prejudged you. You're more like Dr. Dolittle and Louis Pasteur. A doctor, scientist, tenderhearted veterinarian and amazing man."

He pulled her into him, touching her cheek. "God, I do love you, Portia, and while you've mentioned my dating history, I've never said those words to any woman before. I mean it."

"I know you do. You're a man of honor." She pressed her hand to his cheek, the facets in her diamond engagement ring refracting all those little lights into a prism around them.

"So you know I mean every word of this. I love you, with everything that's inside me. I wish I could explain why. I just know that I do—"

She pressed her fingertips to his mouth. "You don't have to explain. I get it."

"You do?"

"I understand what it means to feel something completely irrational and yet very real. Because I'm in love with you, too. In my head I understand we complement each other, our strengths play well to each other. Yet that doesn't matter because I've met other people who fit that criteria and they didn't come close to moving me the way you do with just a look."

"A look?" He eye-stroked her, taking his time.

"Yes, a look." She sidled closer, her body pressed to his. "But I have a little secret for you."

"What would that be?"

"A touch is even better," she whispered in his ear.

He prided himself on being an intelligent man, her very own Louis Pasteur, after all. Although a hint of Tarzan could come in handy every now and again.

He swept an arm behind her knees and lifted her against his chest, sinking with her onto the thick quilt he'd placed there with just this hope in mind.

The hope of celebrating their engagement, their future and their love.

* * * * *

"Just to be clear, this is *not* a date."

Roman shrugged, shooting her a knowing smile. "If you say so. But are you sure this non-date has nothing to do with the fact that you wanted me to kiss you in the library the other day?"

Grace blinked. "When did I say that?"

He grinned. "Sweetheart, you didn't have to. It's been seven years, but I can still read you like a book."

"I seriously doubt that," she said, but her eyes told a different story. Like maybe she worried that he was right. "I'm not the same naive, trusting woman I was back then. And *don't* call me *sweetheart*."

He shrugged. "Sorry, *Gracie*. I thought you liked terms of endearment."

"But that's not why you said it. You're not nearly as charming as you think you are."

"But I *am* charming," he said, waiting for a kick in the shin.

She rolled her eyes instead. "I know you *think* so."

"Honey, I *know* so."

* * *

Back in the Enemy's Bed
is part of the Dynasties: The Newports series—
Passion and chaos consume
a Chicago real-estate empire.